Wokeism on the Rocks

William Scott Anderson

Chapter One

Harold Rock stood facing the wall of glass in his corner office on the 45th floor overlooking the heart of San Fransico. His hands were clasped behind the back of his black tailored suit. He scowled looking down on the city streets far below him. Even from this height, he could still see the tents of the homeless and their endless piles of trash. Harold nearly gagged as his imagination filled his mind with the smell from the last time he was on the street, three weeks ago. He was very careful to stay off the streets of San Fransico as much as possible. Harold drove a luxury car modified to be bullet proof and equipped with several probably illegal defensive systems. He had entered the building through an armored garage door entrance built to stop a 20-ton tank, flanked by armed guards who patrolled the building sidewalks. All of the glass on the first three stories was armored glass. The board had just approved armoring the next three. It was getting harder and harder for employees to get into the building without being robbed, since the indoor parking space was limited. They were in talks to buy the parking garage across the street, secure it and connect it to the building with an enclosed walkway at the 6th floor level. Any lower was thought to be riskier. Many of the employees were still working remotely and were actively resisting any attempts to make them come back to the office. Many of them had moved out of the state of California entirely. The city of San Fransico seemed to be constantly talking about new taxes on businesses to solve the cities problems just like all the previous tax increases were supposed to have done. By rights, by now San Fransico should be a paradise. Lord knows they certainly were paying enough in taxes. By now, every bum on the street should be pretty well off. The money however, simply vanished into city bureaucracy, never to be seen again. It was how all big cities worked. It wasn't what you know, but who you know. Some people knew all the right people. That was the secret of success. He had mastered the game a long time ago. Just then his cell phone rang. He pulled it out of his suit vest pocket and answered it.

"Hello, this is Harold Rock, President of Rock Industries."

"Hello Harold, this is Mayor Paris Graft. I am calling to see if you can help support our clean up the city campaign. Can I count on you for your company to financially support our clean city initiative?"

Harold grimaced, "Absolutely Mayor Graft, you know you can count on us. We are 100% behind you."

"Great, how much can we count on you for?"

He tried to stall. "I will have to check with our financial department to see how much would be prudent at this time."

"Oh, I was hoping you could give me a rough number right away, so we can start making plans based on how much financial backing we have."

"We are 100% behind you Mayor and we will support your initiative fully. I just don't have the numbers in front of me right now. I will have to let you know."

"I hear you are going to buy the parking garage across the street from your building. You do know you will need city approval to build a walkway over the street?"

The claws were starting to come out. He had better feed the cat before she got them all the way out. "I believe we could manage a hundred thousand."

"Now Harold, that isn't very much considering how big your company is. I am sure you can do better."

The cat was hungry today. "Yes Mayor. We are grateful to be able to do business in such a fine city as San Fransico. I think we could do two hundred thousand, and that would be on top of all the other support we give the city."

The cat purred. "Thank you, Harold, I knew I could count on you." Without another word, she hung up. No doubt in a rush to call her next blood donor. Harold wondered what her take was going to be today. He had a feeling it was going to be far more than his. He looked out again at the city and looked back at the phone in his hand.

Harold's wife, Alexandria Rock, swung her arm back over her shoulder and pulled it forward as fast as she could. The brick flew through the air. The large plate glass store window shattered. Glass rained down on the sidewalk. She shouted, "Down with white supremacy! End systemic racism!" She stepped back from the falling glass as the crowd around her surged forward and began grabbing things from the store display. Alexandria smiled in approval as the victims of systemic racism took part of their fair share of the reparations society owed them. She was glad she was able to help them receive partial repayment of the vast debt the world owed them. The world had been built by the labor of slaves and racily suppressed peopled. She picked her sign back up and joined the rest of her group. The descendants of former salves joyfully rushed home to share their bounty with their families. Tonight, they would no doubt share the story of a brave white woman. Who had broken free of the white patriarchy and struck a blow for reparations for the oppressed. She was so pleased with herself, until one of the departing oppressed persons knocked her down. He extended his hand down to help her up. But instead of grabbing her hand, he grabbed her purse and ran off. She got to her feet and looked around at the backs of the fleeing oppressed people, searching for her purse. To her relief, a police car pulled up to the curb right by her. The police officer got out of the car and approached her. "A man stole my purse!"

She heard a voice behind her say, "Now you know how I feel."

She turned and saw the store owner standing behind her, waiting for the cop. He held up his cell phone and showed it to the officer. "She is the one who broke the window, which started the looting."

She stared in shock. "It's not looting! It's reparations for generations of slavery and racism! Hey!" She yelled, as her arms were pulled behind her as the officer put handcuffs on her.

She turned and yelled at the police officer. "You have no right to arrest me!"

The police officer's lip curled just a bit, "Actually, I do."

She struggled and shouted, "Defund the Police! End the white oppression!" as the police officer stuffed her into the back seat of the police car. He got in and started the car. "Now I heard you say your purse was stolen. What would you do if there were no police and your purse was stolen, or worse?"

"I have nothing to fear. Because I help the oppressed." She said smugly.

He asked, "Wasn't that one of the 'oppressed' I saw running away who took your purse?"

"Yes, but I am sure he didn't realize what he was doing, because of all the racism he has faced." She said defensively.

"So, exactly how did you personally racially oppress this guy you never met before?" He said as his lip curled.

"Oh, I have never been a racist. It was white people as group who discriminated against him and oppressed him because of his race." She explained confidently.

"So, you are saying he only took your purse because he saw you as a white person instead as an individual." He said as his lip curled more.

"Yes, that is exactly what happened." She stated as a matter of fact.

"Well, it is clear he discriminated and stole from you, due to your race. Which means he is guilty of racism, and a hate crime." He said as his curl broke out into a full grin.

"Oh, no. That is impossible. Black people have been the victims of racism. They can never be guilty of racism." She explained in surprise.

"Even if they, do it?" He asked innocently.

"No, they could never do it. It is not possible for the oppressed to be the oppressor." She patiently explained.

"Tell that to your missing purse. In my line of work, I see a lot more of black on white crime than white on black crime. Rape too, is pretty much a one-way street as well. If a black is being oppressed by violent crime, it is almost always by another black." He argued logically from his experience as a policeman.

"You're a racist!" She shouted angrily.

"I guess you failed to notice I am black." He said as he grinned widely with more than a bit of humor in his voice.

Alexandria was completely silent for the rest of the trip to the police station.

Harold's son Richard's six-foot four body powered through the water like a torpedo propelled by his powerful masculine muscles leaving all his competitors flailing in his wake. He reached the edge of the pool, grabbed the edge, and leaped up out of the water. He stood proud with water draining off his powerful swimmer's body and raised his hands high over his head in victory as the announcer called out, "Prissy Rock wins the San Fransico College woman's swim meet challenge!" The crowd cheered as many of the female swimmers looked on in dismay.

As Richard left the building, a beautiful college girl his age approached him. "Hey Rock, you stole the win. You only beat my time because you're a man!"

Richard stepped back suddenly causing his dress to sway. He nervously looked around for support but saw Lea had timed this to catch him alone. "Lea, I'm a woman, just like everyone else on the team."

Lea pointed at Richard, "Woman don't have dicks, Dick."

Richard was shocked and flustered. "How dare you deadname me, I am no longer Richard, I have transitioned to Prissy. I am a woman!"

Lea stepped closer and spoke softer, to be sure no one else could hear her. "Richard, you have been brainwashed into thinking your mental problems are from being a 'woman' in a man's body — which is ridiculous. Having a Y chromosome makes you a male and that Y chromosome is in every single cell in your body. Meaning it is genetically impossible for a male to have a woman's brain, since every single cell in your brain has a male Y chromosome."

Richard was flustered, he was not used to being spoken to like this. "I am a woman trapped in a man's body."

Lea cooly continued on. "Genetically, your brain is just as fully male as the rest of you. You don't have a gender problem. You have a mental problem. You are not a woman. You simply have a mental illness. People you trusted, who have a toxic political agenda, have brainwashed a vulnerable mentally ill young man. To use you, to further their agenda of promoting sexual perverts as some sort of protected class of nobility no one is allowed to criticize."

Richard's face turned red. He clinched his fists as his breathing came in a quick series of short breaths as he sucked in oxygen. He drew back his right fist and looked at Lea. But he stopped and looked at the people watching them from a distance. He opened his fist and pointed his finger in Lea's face, shouting loud enough for everyone to hear. "You're transphobic! You're trying to oppress me by misgendering me, that's a crime! I am reporting you to the Dean!"

Richard angerly turned away and marched off towards the Dean's office. Lea's eyes were wide in shock and worry. As she looked around and saw the angry looks many were giving her. She took a quick breath and made a beeline towards her car to get off campus as quickly as possible. She realized Richard had put a rather large target on her back. The Dean would probably expel her. She saw a girl with blue hair and facial piercings, point at her and shout, "trans rights are human rights!" Lea turned away from her and broke into a run. Another girl with face tattoos swung at her as she ran by, hitting her shoulder. She staggered from the blow but regained her stride. She saw the next blow coming and managed to dodge it. It only grazed her face. With tears running down her cheeks, she made it to her parked car and quickly got in, locking the door. Quickly she buckled up and started the car. She backed out, turned to leave. She looked back, the crowd was moving towards her car. She pressed down the accelerator, heading out of the lot before they could reach her. She drove off campus since it would probably be too dangerous to go back to her dorm and pack. She considered her actions, deciding her best and safest course was to just keep driving until she was safely back at her parents' house. She started her long cross-country drive; very happy her parents didn't live in the state.

Harold's daughter, Amelia, Sat at a table by herself in the high school lunchroom eating her lunch. Her childhood friend, Mary Jane, sat down across from her. Amelia smiled at her. "Hi Andromeda, how are you doing today. I love your hair."

Mary Jane padded her blue afro style perm. It made her head look like a giant blue dandelion gone to seed. "Thanks Pandora, I think it came out very well. Nobody misses me when I walk into a room."

Amelia looked envious and sighed. "Oh, I would love that. So far, my superpower seems to be invisibility. No one in my family even notices if I am around, if they are ever home."

Mary Jane looked at Amelia's top. "I like your non-binary gender symbol. What did your parents think of it?"

"I think they would have to notice me before they could notice it. Our maid saw it and asked if I was going to a Catholic school."

Mary Jane giggled. "Why would she ask that?"

Amelia rolled her eyes. "She said that if you turn it upside down, it looks like a symbol for the Pope."

Mary Jane covered her mouth with her hand as she tried to suppress her laughter. "Considering what the

Pope has been saying about non-binary people, it may make some sense. But I hear Catholics are wondering is if the Pope is Catholic."

Amelia pointed at the symbol on her chest and spoke. "I certainly don't know what I am or what I want to be. I find this whole thing so confusing, and my parents are no help at all. My big brother thinks he is a girl and has joined the girls swim team. But I wonder if he just did it because he couldn't win against men swimmers, so he decided it would be easier to beat up the girls instead. While my parents act like it's a good thing and say he is so brave. But I think he needs to see a shrink."

Mary Jane was shocked. "Pandora, how can you say that? Your brother is very brave to come out as a transwoman and is an example for everyone. You should be ashamed of yourself!"

Amelia leaned back and took in a sudden breath of air and tried hard not to cry. "Sorry Andromeda, I didn't think of it that way. I guess I must try to stop thinking of him as my big brother and try to start thinking of him as my big sister."

Mary Jane glared at her. "HER, HER! You need get her pronouns right. You also have to get your own pronouns right too. You can't let people use female pronouns for you, when you are non-binary."

Amelia looked abashed. "Yes, Andromeda, you are right. I will do that. I understand what you are saying. We have been friends since preschool. I don't want to lose you. I would really miss you. I think of you like my sister."

Mary Jane coldly pointed out, "Pandora, you already have a sister. Did you forget already?"

Amelia looked worried. "No, I just have a hard time trying to think of my brother as my sister. I just find this so confusing. You remember why I changed my name to Pandora? It was because inside me, my life is filled with problems no one else can see, unless I open up to them. I just need help to sort things out."

Mary Jane looked around. "Everybody has their own problems. You just need to deal with yours." With that, she got up and walked away without looking back. Amelia felt a tear roll down her cheek and brushed it off with her finger. She looked at the tear on her fingertip, and wondered why it was there. What was it Andromeda said that made her want to cry?

Chapter Two

Harold Rock drove through the streets of San Fransico, with trepidation. But for once, it was not about driving in San Fransico, it was about where he was going. He headed north and got on freeway 80 and took the San Francisco – Oakland Bay Bridge. His theory was, the reason why most of the people like himself paid so much money to live in crime infested San Fransico, was so they wouldn't have to live in Oakland. It was probably the only place in the entire country which made San Fransico, look like a better place to live. He knew most people thought the reason why you only had to pay the toll going into San Fransico, was it was like an admission fee. But he suspected the actual reason was they knew people would definitely be willing to pay money to get out of Oakland.

Due to the on-going implosion of local government, the Oakland Glenn Dyer Detention Facility jail was closed. He had to drive all the way to the Alameda County Santa Rita Jail way out in Dublin. Even without traffic it was an over an hour drive, with traffic, it would probably be a lot longer.

Two hours later, he arrived at the jail, and parked in the assigned parking space. He called a number on his cell phone and waited nearly another hour, before his wife came out the gate. She got in the car and said, "Let's get out of here."

He replied, "Sure thing, but not too fast, I don't want to be guest here."

Alexandria turned and looked at him. "Not funny Harold. We also need to pick up the car. It's in a lot in downtown Oakland across the street from where I was arrested."

Harold rolled his eyes. He said gruffly, "You have got to be kidding me. It will be dark soon and you want to go to downtown Oakland?"

Alexandria was tired and angry. "We have to pick up the car Harold."

"The car is replaceable, we are not. The odds are it's already gone. But I am willing to give it a try. But if it looks iffy, we get out of dodge as quickly as we can."

"Harold, Oakland is filled with repressed people. We are not their oppressors. We just explain it to them, and everything will be fine."

Harold just grumped and drove the car into the city center business area. Alexandria directed him towards the lot. "There it is that's the lot."

He turned into the lot and switched to high beams looking the lot over carefully as he entered. He didn't see anyone as he drove slowly into the lot. "Where is the car parked? I don't see it."

"Harold, it's right over there, behind that van." she said angerly.

They drove past the van, but the next spot was empty.

"I don't understand it, I parked it right there!" She said confused and angry.

Harold pulled a spotlight from a holder under the dash and shined it out on the pavement. It sparkled with broken glass on the left side of the parking space. "I see broken glass on the ground. Looks like they broke the driver side window and drove it off." He said logically.

Before Alexandria could reply, several young black males surrounded the car. One of them, standing next to the driver's door, had a gun pointed at Harold's head. What happened next happened very quickly. Harold flipped open a hidden panel on the center console, teargas sprayed out in a fog around the car. The car accelerated quickly in reverse over a speed bump shooting backwards out onto the street. Harold threw it into drive and hit the gas hard as they raced away from the parking lot. Once they were a block away, Harold slowed down and got back on the freeway taking the bridge back to San Fransico. After they were over the bridge, Harold actually felt safer being in San Fransico, which was a weird feeling but that was the magic of the Oakland effect.

It was late when they reached their driveway. Harold used his car remote to open the gate and drove in. He let the gate close behind them and stopped the car. He got out and walked back to the control for the gate. Harold used the keypad to lock out the remote in his wife's car. He checked the entry log, saw both kids were home and the help had left for the night.

He parked in the Garage. They walked into the house. Amelia was lying on the couch playing on her phone. She looked up, "Serenity left dinner in the fridge, said you can warm it up when you get home."

Alexandria looked in the fridge and pulled out the foil covered pans. She checked the contents, put them in the already preheated oven and set the timer. Seeing the table was set, she went to take a shower. While Harold went to his home office's computer to check the market closings and review the financial reports on the tottering global economy.

Later the timer went off. Harold pulled the hot pans out of the oven. He set them on the stove top and peeled back the foil. He filled a plate and took it to his office. Amelia filled a plate and sat down at the dining room table, alone. Richard smelled the food and piled it on a plate like he was loading a cargo ship, then sailed back to his room. Alexandria filled a plate and filled a large glass with wine. She took it into the rec-room and put a show on. Amelia looked around the empty dining room with a sad face, slowly eating in silence.

Harold, while on the computer, pulled out his cell phone. He made a call to someone in the police department, with whom he had a financial arrangement with, and reported the stolen car. His contact agreed to fill out the reports for him so he could proceed with the insurance claim, since the police would probably not even look for the car. All of this was as Harold expected until his contact said, "Harold, you have to get out of town tomorrow."

Harold was puzzled. "Why? What is going on?"

"Listen, you are not the only one I help out. Some people help me out, and let me know things. There is going to be a big BLM -Antifa double header, day after tomorrow. The plan is they are going to loot and burn the upper-class homes where you live."

Harold felt his blood run cold. "Does the mayor and the chief of police know about this? I am wondering if it is time to call in some favors and get a swat team out here to protect the neighborhood."

In a lowered voice, as if afraid his boss would walk in, he said, "You know, this could never happen without their approval. They already got their marching orders on this. They are removing all the police from the area. This is coming from Washington. They want this to happen for the next national election."

Harold's left hand tightened into a fist. "Sounds like you are right about getting out of town. Thanks for the warning, you will be seeing something extra from me. I know who my friends are."

After they ended the phone call, Harold immediately placed another call to his flight service. "This is Harold Rock. I would like my private jet fueled and prepped for a flight tomorrow to Hawaii. Yes, and please notify my pilot. . . Probably about noon."

After he got off the phone, he went to the rec-room just as Amelia walked into the room. Alexandria was finishing her third class of wine. "Something big has come up. I need to go to Hawaii tomorrow. I want to take the whole family along. I thought we could all use a vacation." He said, with what he hoped was a convincing smile.

Amelia nearly jumped for joy. It had been years since they had gone on a family vacation. Alexandria, feeling warm and at peace from the wine, said, "That would be marvelous. I always enjoy seeing the Redwood trees."

Harold just nodded and went to inform his son. He knocked at his door, Richard said, "Come in."

Harold opened the door and found his son sitting at a vanity putting on makeup. There were more makeup containers in front of him than Harold could count. His son looked like an over the hill, lady of the night, who thought makeup was the fountain of youth.

"Good thing you don't smoke. You got so much of that stuff on, if it is the least bit flammable, you would go up in a puff of smoke."

"Dad, I thought you supported my transitioning." He replied irritably.

"You know I support what every you want to do with your life. Just don't light yourself on fire. Look, I wanted to tell you, we are going to Hawaii tomorrow. I want you along too." He said with appeasement.

Richard stopped as if some had hit a pause button. "You want me along?"

"Yes, I do."

"Sure Dad."

"You can pack in the morning. We take off at noon."

Next morning Harold woke up late. The sun had been up for hours, the bedroom was bright from the mid-morning sun. Alexandria was snoring loudly next to him. He got up, got dressed, packed a suitcase. He got a suitcase for his wife and laid it out open, so she would remember to pack when she got up.

He left the bedroom and went downstairs. He found Amelia sitting on the couch with her suitcase sitting on the floor. Next to it, sat another larger packed suitcase. It was a more feminine one, so he knew it was Richard's. "Glad to see both of you are packed."

He went into the kitchen to look for Richard and found him sitting at the table while Serenity was cooking breakfast. She was a tall strong black woman with equally strong opinions. "I is so mad this morning! Last night some rich white man ran over an innocent black man, out walking with his friends. Then when they axed him to drive him to the hospital, he dishes them with teargas and takes off. A hit and run, that is why there is so much crime in Oakland, white people! We otta lock you'all up."

"Maybe after breakfast Serenity, what are you cooking this morning?" Harold asked, hoping not to set her off, while trying not to think of what her reaction would be if she found out about his recent adventure in Oakland.

"Can't you see what Prissy is eating? Or did your eyes fall out of your head? Now do you want some or not." Serenity said loudly with one hand on her hip while she waved the spatula around in the air like a sword.

Harold sat down across from Richard who was wearing a tropical flowered dress. "I will have what he, I mean SHE, is having."

Serenity pointed the spatula at him. "Good choice, that is what we gots."

She started cracking eggs and dropping them one by one on the griddle. As they fried, she threw more bacon on and put more bread in the toaster. "More white bread for the white folk." She mumbled.

Gabriela, the maid, came in dropping her purse on the counter. "How about some breakfast Serenity? I got a late start his morning and had to leave without breakfast."

Serentiy turned to glare at her and angerly said, "I get paid to cook for the white folks, not some lazy assed Mexican."

Both of Gabriela's hands went straight to her hips. Her elbows waved back and forth like they were wings as if she was a bird trying to take off as she angerly retorted, "Lazy! Lazy! Mexicans do all the work in this country. Just look around, everywhere it is us doing all the hard labor jobs, agriculture, landscaping, construction, factory jobs, nearly all done by Hispanics and Mexicans. What do the lazy blacks do? Do they work hard and make money, no they steal and rob us! Everybody knows black neighborhoods are the most dangerous parts of town, even the blacks don't want to live there!"

Serentiy's left hand was back on her hip with her right pointing the spatula. She looked like a rotating battleship gun turret, as she turned to point at Gabriela and fired off her angry response. "It all because of white oppression, slavery, discrimination, that blacks can't get good jobs! It is white people doing all the crime and blaming it on innocent black people. White cops are always arresting us and throwing us into prisons. Once we get our reparations for slavery and discrimination, I will own this house and the Rocks will be my slaves and work for me!"

Gabriela elbows waved violently as she fired back. "Reparations? For what! Do you even know the names of any of your ancestors who are actually slaves? Were they even mistreated? Did they even want to be free? For all you know they may have been hardworking happy slaves, who would see blacks today as lazy and worthless trash."

Serentiy pointed the spatula up and then sharply brought it down to point at Gabriela for emphasis as she fired off each of her points, like a ship's gun recoiling after each shot. "All blacks are descended from slaves! We is all discriminated against by white people! White people owe us! ...The Rocks owe me this house for me having to slave away here for them! When all I gots a ghetto apartment!"

Gabriela who was shorter than Serentiy, accented each of her points by rising up on her toes to look her in the eye, as she flapped her elbows. But this made her look like a bird hopping to get off the ground. "It is their house because they paid for it and you didn't! Not all blacks come from slavery, some come from other countries! Why should you get money for something that happened long ago to someone you can't even name! You only live in a ghetto because it is a black neighborhood, if it was a Hispanic neighborhood, it would be a nice place to live! It is not the location; it's the people!"

The spatula slowly dropped to point at the floor. Serentiy looked like she had taken a hit and stopped firing as she tried to think of what to fire back with. After a moment, she turned on a dime, and sailed away to break off the engagement, while firing a departing salvo over her shoulder. "Black people have problems because of white people."

Gabriela got ready to go to work and fired her parting shot. "Reparations wouldn't fix anything. It would be a one-time thing that no matter how large, would be blown away in no time and gone. Capitalism is the problem. You have to fix the system. The workers should all share equally in redistribution of the wealth. Fair wages for all. Then everyone will be rich, and I will have this house after the revolution." She turned and left to start cleaning.

Once Gabriela left the room, Serentiy served Harold his breakfast. Which he ate quietly since he didn't feel like he could say anything without being called racist or white privileged. It was the no win situation he had learned to live with.

Later, Richard helped Harold put the suitcases in the trunk of the car. Harold tried to check the back of the car for any traces from the night before, without Richard noticing, but he didn't see anything.

When he went back in the house, Alexandria was up and eating breakfast watching news on the TV. He asked her, "Are you all packed?"

She was staring at the TV as she distractedly said, "Yes, it's on the bed upstairs. Is that our neighbor's house down the street?"

He turned and looked at the screen in shock and hurriedly said, "I will get your bag in the car." He rushed upstairs. As he passed Gabriela moving the vacuum cleaner, he said, "We are leaving for vacation now, so you are on vacation with pay until we return. There seems to be a riot coming up the street, so now would be a very good time to leave."

Gabriela simply turned and put the vacuum back in the closest and headed out. Harold grabbed his wife's suitcase and rushed out and put it in the car. He then rushed into the kitchen and told Serentiy who was out the back kitchen door before Harold was even out of the kitchen. By now the kids were watching the TV as well, having heard Harold rushing about telling the staff to go home. Harold took a moment to evaluate the situation. The drone footage seemed to be live. It was an air shot of the end of the street. The mob was made up of Antifa and BLM supporters who were climbing over a gate and throwing rocks at the windows of a house. Smoke and flames were soon pouring out. A pickup truck plowed through the gate and the crowd poured in. The view swung to show more of the mob moving up the street towards their house. Harold knew they had to act fast. "Got the bags in the car, time to go."

The kids headed to the car while Alexandria looked puzzled and asked, "Why are they doing this? We never did anything to them?"

Harold stepped quickly over to her and took her by the hand. "We can talk about it in the car. We must go now." He gently but firmly pulled on her hand, pulling her up off the couch. Once she was standing, he put his right hand around her and took her left hand in his and pushed her along as he guided her to the door. Once in the garage, he nearly pushed her into the passenger seat and leaned in to buckle her in. Slamming her car door, he raced around and got in. He started the car and used the remote to open the garage door. They were already there. Harold saw the mob leaders in their back Antifa outfits on the driveway blocking them. He reached into the center console, pressed a button, and put the car in drive. The men in their black masked military looking uniforms, prepared to intercept the car, blocking them. Harold eased the car forward out of the garage. They leaned forward to put their hands on the car to stop him. But as soon as they did that, they recoiled in pain from the electric shock defense system. Harold used the moment to increase his speed. Some got out of the way, while one pulled out a handgun and started shooting. Harold flinched as the bullets hit the car. The windshield held, but bullet marks appeared in the glass. Alexandria screamed in terror and Harold put the petal to the metal. Bodies went flying everywhere as they tried to jump out of the way of the speeding car as more bullets were fired at the car. Harold hit the remote for the gate which obediently started to open, despite the number of people who were climbing over it. The crowd in the street rushed towards the opening gate. Harold raced down the short driveway toward the gate as the gate climbers tumbled off on both sides as the gate crashers in the street charged toward them. The gate did manage to open fully, much to Harold's relief. He put the petal back down. The car engine roared. The car surged forward as Harold pressed the teargas button and held it down. The teargas sprayed out in all directions. The mob backed off. Harold thought he would be able to make it to the street. But Some of the more aggressive big guys in the mob tried to tackle the car, like line backers swarming a quarterback. It went epically wrong as they charged. They got a face full of teargas and when they hit the car, the electric shock, threw them off onto the ground. They ended up rolling in pain on the ground, blinded by the teargas as they choked on the fumes.

The mob in the street saw what was coming and most tried to get out of the way, while a few threw bricks and rocks at the car. Some hit the car with bats as it passed but got teargassed in return. Those with aluminum bats got an extra surprise. The car was battered as they went through the BLM-Antifa gantlet. The crowd soon thinned out. Harold switched off the teargas. He increased speed to get out of the neighborhood and away from any more rioters.

They got on 101 and headed south to the San Fransico International Airport. Harold was really trying to stay focused on driving, since there was a lot of traffic and most of the drivers thought traffic laws were for other people. He gritted his teeth. The traffic was nearly as bad as Seattle. His family were slowly coming out of the daze they were in. The experience had been quite a shock for them. Richard asked, "Dad, how were you able to do that?"

Harold smiled. "Not my first time. One of my secrets is that I went to college on the GI bill. Had a tour in the army. Had a situation very much like today, but probably still classified."

Richard was puzzled by this. "Why didn't you ever mention any of this."

Harold tried hard to keep his mind on driving as the car which had just cut him off gave him a free brake check. "First thing I learned in college, never ever let anyone find out you were ex-military. Also learned about camouflage and the art of blending in. Never put a target on yourself."

Richard was intrigued. "Dad you really got to tell me more about this."

Harold was very distracted by driving. "Yes son, we can talk on the plane. Not while I am trying to drive a two-ton armored car through heavy traffic on the freeway. This is more dangerous than driving on our street was."

Chapter Three

One of the best things about the San Fransico airport, is it isn't in San Fransico. It's well south of the city, which allowed it to operate fairly well. Of course, the SFPD had to guard the airport terminal from homeless people using the BART system to go sleep in the airport at night. Harold, wasn't going to the airport terminal. He went to the parking lot for his air service. They parked and walked in. Immediately they were walked to the hanger where Harold's plane was stored. The lady leading them checked her tablet. "Your jet has been fully fueled and serviced. Galley services have been fully stocked. Your pilot is in the ready room and is on his way over. I just need to have you sign here. This is the total charges here."

Harold looked at the astronomical figure. It didn't faze him. Owning a private jet was like flying with the doors and windows open while the plane was stuffed full of loose hundred-dollar bills blowing out in the wind. He signed and smiled. A huge guy in a pilot's uniform walked up and introduced himself. "I am Captain Muhammad Aman Allah. It is a pleasure to be your pilot today. I see we are flying to Hawaii. Can I assist you in getting your bags on board?"

He helped them get their bags up the stairs. Alexandria stepped up one step, held her suitcase out and Muhammad took it. Next, she held out her hand for

Muhammad to help her up the stairs. But Muhammad pulled back his hand, put it on his chest and said, "Right this way, my lady" He stepped back out of the way. Alexandria was dumbfounded and looked at Harold. Harold waved her on. She climbed the steps into the plane.

Richard did the same. But when Muhammad reached down for his suitcase, he froze with a look of complete horror on his face. As he realized Richard was actually a man in a dress. Muhammad struggled internally for several long seconds. His face underwent a series of rapid contortions as he struggled trying to regain control of his emotions and his composure. Flashing across his out-of-control facial muscles, where brief violent flashes of horror, anger, revulsion, disgust, dismay, fear, worry, determination and finally an attempted professional smile which flickered like a light that might not stay on. He did manage to take Richard's bag and said, "Right this way . . ."

Amelia climbed the stairs next and held up her bag with a smile. Muhammad looked down with a forced smile. But he relaxed and his smile became real when he realized that Amelia was a real woman or rather a girl in her case. He took her bag and said, "Right this way, young lady."

Harold climbed up the stairs with his suitcase and entered the cabin. Muhammad said, "Welcome aboard, sir."

Muhammad stored their bags in the back of the plane and got them all seat belted in. He gave them the safety instructions and said, "We will be taking off shortly, enjoy your flight." He went into the cockpit and closed the door.

The hanger doors opened. A pushback tug came in, pulled the jet out of the hanger, and took it to the taxiway. It disconnected and left. Muhammad started the engines, checked his displays and released the brake once he was cleared to taxi towards the runway. Soon he was cleared for takeoff. The jet shot down the runway and pulled up into the sky. Harold watched out the window as they turned to the west and flew out over the ocean.

Harold was sitting next to his wife. He turned on the entertainment screen checking for any news on the riot. He soon saw drone footage of the riot. Smoke was rising from burning mansions. The streets were filled with people fighting over things looted from the burning homes. His wife was sobbing and shaking. He put his arm around her shoulders and held her. He spotted some homes of people he knew, not all of them jerks. He was shocked by this turn of events. The scene cut to a black car crashing through the crowd while blowing white fog. The audio said, "Police are searching for the driver of a black car, who attacked the mostly peaceful protesters. Ramming into the crowd causing many injuries while teargassing hundreds of peaceful demonstrators. The protesters were unsuccessful in their attempts to protect themselves from this attack of terror, despite using bricks and bats to ward off the attacking car. The driver also reportedly electrocuted many of the people in the crowd by using some kind of high voltage electric attack that struck people with lightning bolts, ten or even twenty feet away. There are reports that the car was bullet proof. The San Fransico Police Depart Swat Team was unable to stop the car in a fierce firefight on the freeway. The far-right terrorist driver has so far escaped capture. This attack is also believed to be connected to a hate crime attack on a black man in Oakland last night involving a vehicle with a very similar distribution which also used teargas. It was this earlier attack last night which trigged the mostly peaceful protest today. The San Fransico District Attorney's Office has already issued an arrest warrant for the believed driver of the high-tech terror car, Elon Musk. Anyone with information about the location of Elon Musk or his terror car, is encouraged to call the San Fransico Police Department. Anyone triggered by the terrorist events portrayed in this report can call the California Department of Health Care Services CalHOPE Warm Line for emotional support counseling provided free by the state of California. Due to high call volumes, wait times can exceed 24 hours."

Harold turned the screen off as he darkly thought about how things had changed. One moment he was a highly successful businessman, and the next he was a terrorist sought by the police. He wondered what Elon Musk thought about this. On the other hand, Elon Musk was probably used to it by now. He was beginning to see maybe why Elon Musk wanted to go to Mars. He wished he had some place he could go to get away from it all. He knew Hawaii was probably not going to be far enough. His thoughts were interrupted by Richard asking a question.

"Dad, what happened back there. I saw the news videos. How were you able to do it?" Richard asked sincerely.

Harold kept his arm around Alexandria and looked back at Richard who was in the seat behind her. "As you know, things have been getting really dangerous in San Fransico for years now. There is a company in Mexico that does bulletproof conversions on cars. You can also order some security extras. It seemed like a wise precaution. One I might say which came in very handy today. It is one purchase I will never regret." He said with feeling.

Richard asked, "How did you end up in the army?"

Harold said, "Well there isn't much to tell. My father had been an army guy and wanted his son to be one as well. I mainly did it for the GI bill, to pay for college. The army, or any military service for that matter, is something most people would rather forget about. The only guys I met who liked the military had never been shot at. That is why I never talked about it. I found out really quick in college it was very much frowned on if not outright hated."

Richard was surprised. "You were shot at? What happened?"

Harold suddenly looked older. "Like I said, I don't talk about it. Never press a veteran to talk about it if he doesn't want to. You don't want to know. It would probably give you bad dreams."

Richard was a bit confused. "But how did you end up a liberal? Your company is one of the greenest liberal companies in the world."

Harold chuckled. "It started in college. Everything in college was liberal. I very much wanted to fit in and succeed, so I became a liberal. The truth was, at first, I was only pretending to get by. But the longer you pretend, the more real it becomes. If you wear a disguise long enough, after a while, you can't take it off, it becomes the real you."

Richard asked another question. "But what about your company? Why did you make it liberal?"

Harold smirked. "Just like I had to pretend to be a liberal in college, my company has to do the same to get government contracts and public approval."

"How does that work Dad?"

Harold's smirk got bigger. "Time to let you in on the family business secret. Most of our manufacturing is done in China and such places, like everyone else. Competition is not based on lower costs, or better quality, but on greenwashing and virtue signaling. For example, we have had cost increases in our consumer products division, and we had to raise prices which could result in reduced sales. What we did was change the packaging to a green save the earth theme design, with a claim that our products were some certain percent less polluting than the old products. While not telling anyone the old products we based the comparison on, were banned years ago for being too harmful to the environment. The other trick was to raise the price several times the actual cost increase, which greatly increased our profit margin. The consumers saw our products as a more expensive, better for the environment product. They would buy our products and brag about it on social media to virtue signal to all their friends which increased our sales even more."

Richard was impressed. "I can see how that would work very well. But is it all there is to running your company?"

Harold explained further. "That is just the kindergarten stuff. Greenwashing allows you to build up a green environmental score. The green image opens the door to government contracts and other deals. Once you get into government sales, you really need to know how to play the game of paying off the right people. Government procurement is not really about getting the best product, but rather the best bribe. As they say, there isn't a single politician who can climb a rope, because they have all had their palms greased."

Richard was confused. "Dad, that can't be true. You are not seeing the real world."

Harold shook his head and sadly said. "But I am son. My secret is I am all about the money. I am a realist. I do whatever works. If I didn't have to bribe people, I certainly wouldn't, since it would be a waste of money."

Richard asked, "What are you really Dad?"

Harold looked into his son's eyes, trying hard to ignore the eyeliner. "I am a liberal who is a closeted realist."

Richard thought about that and asked, "Why are you a closeted realist, can't you come out?"

Harold chuckled. "I learned in my college days, liberals hate realists. Liberals live in their own imaginary world. It's why they attack anyone who threatens to pop the soap bubble they live in. So, I hid my realism, like our car which saved our lives."

Richard was shocked, "But Dad, what you did was illegal!"

"How? Was I wrong to save my family? Did I attack anyone? All my actions were defensive, maybe reckless and dangerous, but necessary to save our lives."

Richard looked thoughtful. "You are right Dad. Thank you for saving us. What you did was incredible. I could never do anything like it."

Harold in a fatherly way said, "You are younger, stronger, and probably smarter than me. You can probably do even better."

Richard was surprised by the praise from his father. It had been a very eventful day, and it would be a long time before they got to Hawaii. Richard reclined his seat and relaxed. He soon drifted off to sleep. Harold noticed Alexandria was out sound, and probably had been for some time. He slipped his arm out from behind her, turned and saw Amelia was out as well. He leaned back his seat and napped.

The pilot, Captain, Muhammad Aman Allah was now the only one awake on the plane. Having served in the Pakistan Air Force, where pilots were selected based on how highly connected they were, rather than skilled, he was not the best pilot. He had also lied on his application form, greatly exaggerating his flying hours and skills. He had never learned how to use the jet's advanced GPS navigation system. He followed the old school way of navigating, following the roads and coastlines. Muhammad was actually rather good at spotting landmarks on the ground and knowing where he was. The only problem was you can't see Hawaii from California, not even at the highest altitude the jet could achieve, which he had just discovered. But it was not a problem, he simply aimed the jet towards where Hawaii should be and flew towards it. With help from Allah, he was sure to find his way, since once he was closer, he would be able to see Hawaii from high in the air.

Harold stirred and opened his eyes. It didn't seem like it was much later. They were flying west and racing with the sun, which made the day longer. He pulled out his phone and checked the time, which was confusing since cell phones update to the time zone as you travel. He checked west coast time, and discovered it was eight PM. They should have landed two hours ago. He got up and used the bathroom and got something to eat from the galley. He took a prepared roast beef sub back to his seat and sat down. He ate it and picked up the intercom phone by his seat. He called the pilot.

Muhammad was very worried, where was Hawaii? He should have seen it hours ago. There had been some clouds. He didn't know if he had unknowingly flown right over it, or if he had missed it by enough, it had been over the horizon even at this altitude. It could still be just ahead of him if the jet steam had held him back. He fervently prayed to Allah it was still ahead of him. He desperately searched the horizon for Hawaii. The intercom buzzed and startled him badly. He looked around in a panic for any red lights. Finally, he saw the blinking light on the intercom. He picked it up. Harold asked, "Captain Allah, will we be landing soon? We have been in the air for a long time."

Muhammad trying hard to suppress his nervousness said, "We have been flying against the jet stream, it has taken longer than expected. We should be landing in about an hour."

"Thank you, captain, could I bring you anything from the galley?"

"No thanks, I already ate." They said their goodbyes and hung up. Allah wondered if maybe he had missed Hawaii while he was in the bathroom. He really needed more fiber in his diet.

After an hour and half, Harold was getting concerned. This was his jet, and he knew the fuel tanks only held enough for about ten hours of flight. They had been in the air for nine and half hours and they had not even begun to descend. He picked up the intercom and called again.

Muhammad still couldn't see Hawaii. He nervously checked the fuel gage. He still had enough, hopefully. The intercom buzzing made him sweat. He picked it up.

Harold tried to phrase his words very carefully asked. "Captain Allah, how does it look up there. Everything going well?"

In voice just a bit higher than normal, Muhammad tried to speak with his best captain's voice. "We are approaching our destination and will be landing soon. I will soon be putting the seatbelt sign on for landing. Please put away any loose things in preparation for landing." He hung up the intercom since he really didn't know what else to say. Looking off at the horizon, he finally saw land. His spirits rose as he turned the jet toward it.

Harold felt the small turn and assumed they were getting close, even though he still couldn't see anything but water below them.

The land on the horizon grew larger as he approached. But it just completely refused to grow into the state of Hawaii, which was a complete disappointment to Muhammad. He could see many more small islands scattered beyond the first one, but none of them were Hawaii. Maybe the Rocks would be happy with landing on one of them. Being stupid rich Americans, they probably couldn't tell a fancy hotel on one island from another, as long as it had a good bar. It would not matter. They would get so drunk, in the morning he could find out which way Hawaii was, and fly them there, before their hangovers wore off. He looked the islands over trying to pick out one which looked like it was big enough for a big hotel. But the low fuel warning light came on. Muhammad decided it was the will of Allah they land on the first island, since it was closest.

Harold relaxed as he felt the plane begin to descend. It was about time. It had never taken this long to get to Hawaii before.

Muhammad looked over the island Allah had chosen. He was getting concerned because he had not spotted the airport yet. Some island airports could be hard to find. He turned on the radio and made a general call to airport control, since he didn't know which island he was approaching. He didn't get any answer. He switched to another common approach frequency and tried again. After he worked through several possible frequencies with no radio traffic or replies, he became concerned. He was much closer to the island at a much lower altitude and had yet to see any roads or buildings. He was very worried when the emergency fuel warning came on with a red flashing light and a repeating audio warning. "Low fuel, Low fuel!" He prayed to Allah. When he opened his eyes, he saw the answer to his prayers, there was the runway right in front of him. He turned on the seatbelt signs, but didn't make an announcement, since he didn't want them to hear the low fuel warning.

He turned to line up on the runway and descended. It was a long white runway running right along the edge of the water. He fully extended his landing flaps and throttled the engines back as the wheels touched down. The wheels grabbed much more than he expected and jerked the plane hard as it slowed down faster than it normally would have. Muhammad was thrown forward against his restraints as the plane plowed to a stop, but not quite. Muhammad looked ahead and saw the runway had a large white rock in the middle of it. The nose of the jet cleared the rock, but the landing gears and engines didn't. He felt the forward gear go as it was smashed off with a jarring jolt. Followed by the main two gears with a much bigger jolt which was hard enough that no one had noticed the engines getting smashed against the rock at same time. Being an experienced pilot, Muhammad turned on the PA and said, "Welcome to Hawaii."

Chapter Four

Harold and his family were tossed and shaken by the very rough landing. Harold's first thought was, "That dam incompetent diversity hire pilot just wreaked my plane!"

Muhammad came out of cockpit and tried to open the boarding door, but it was stuck. He leaned into it and rammed it with his shoulder and managed to force it open. It flipped out and down, but not all the away. The stairs on the inside of the door were at too shallow of an angle since the ground was a lot closer due to the jet no longer having any wheels. He next got their suitcases and dropped them out the door on the ground.

While he was doing this, Harold was checking to see if his family was all right. Richard was looking out the window and said "The wing looks broken. I think we landed on the beach."

Alexandria stood up and stretched her back. "Let's get a cab, and get to a hotel. It has been a long day."

Amelia got out of her seat, ran and put her arms around Harold. "Daddy, we crashed!"

Harold patted her back. "Yes. we did sweetheart. But we get to walk away from this one. Speaking of which, we should get outside right away." With that he led them off the plane. Once they were outside looking back at the crashed plane, Muhammad came over.

Harold glared at him. "Captain Allah, where are we?"

Muhammad said, "Hawaii."

Harold tried again. "Where in Hawaii are we?'

Muhammad looked around. "We were running out of fuel on final approach. We had to do an emergency landing on the beach."

Harold asked again. "Where is this beach located."

Muhammad didn't bat an eye. "East coast of the Big Island, just east of Hilo International Airport. Should be just over there. I can stay with the plane and report the accident. You can take your bags, walk to the terminal, and get a cab."

Harold looked at Richard who shook his head. Harold said, "Let's grab our bags and take a look."

Muhammad nodded his head enthusiastically. "Yes! Yes! Do that, walk to the terminal!"

He helped them get their suitcases and they started walking inland away from the plane toward the airport. They struggled with the suitcases since the roller wheels were useless on sand. They ended up carrying them. Once they were up on the top edge of the beach away from the plane, they stopped to look around for the airport. Richard spoke to Harold. "I was looking out the window as we came in. This is a small island, not the big island. Dad, I never saw an airport and I didn't see anything on this island as we came in."

Harold set his suitcase down and looked around. "We are not in Kansas anymore, and we certainly are not in Hawaii. Unless this is one of the small islands. But I don't think so, or we would have seen one of the bigger islands as we came in."

Harold looked back at his plane. It really was a wreck. He saw Muhammad go back inside the plane. "I think, I will go back to the plane and make sure Captain Allah sends a distress signal, so somebody can come get us, or we could be here a long time." Harold along with his family were knocked to the ground by the sudden wall of wind from the bright orange explosive fireball rising from where the plane had been.

Harold's ears were ringing but he couldn't hear anything. He struggled back to his feet and found the world to be a very different place than it was a moment ago. In front of them was a fire storm of burning fuel with aluminum metal pieces raining down out of the sky. He threw his right arm over his head as a shield. Even from this distance he could feel the intense heat of the fire. His family were all dazed and deafened as he was. But he managed to get them to take their things and move back away from the intense heat of the fire. Once off the sand of the beach, there was the back edge of a sand dune, which shielded them from the heat. They sat down on their suitcases and rested. Harold looked around at the forest or jungle that grew down to the beach. Beyond which he had seen a hill or small peak when they came in. He wondered what they were going to do.

The fire burned very hot for less than an hour, died down and went out. Harold took Richard with him. They went down to check on what was left. Richard still in sandals and a woman's tropical dress, asked, "What do you think we will find?"

Harold was grim. "Probably not much. But we must look. I think our captain went up in smoke with the plane. But there may be something left we can use. Like an emergency radio or food and water. But it probably all burned."

They walked toward the blacken rock the plane had crashed on, through sand covered with pieces of blackened metal blown off the plane by the explosion. Harold flinched when he saw something white, but it was only an aluminum spar from the plane. Most of the plane was gone. Just burned fragments remained. Harold was relieved they hadn't found any of the remains of the pilot. But was disappointed they hadn't found anything useful.

He and Richard headed back to the girls. Amelia was leaning up against Alexandria, who had her arm around her and was stroking her hair. Amelia was leaning into it like a kitten who really wanted to be petted. Alexandria looked at Harold and said, "Call us a cab to take us to the hotel."

Harold pulled out his phone and checked his reception. "No cell reception here. I can't get anything."

Richard said, "Same here."

Alexandria irritably said, "Well then, you will just have to walk over to the hotel and get a cab for us."

Harold threw his arms out. "There is nothing here. It looks like no one lives on this island. We didn't see any buildings or roads as we landed."

Alexandria was having trouble processing this. Confused she asked, "Well, where are we going to get a room for the night then?"

Harold spread his arms out. "You are looking at it."

Alexandria gasped. "You have got to be kidding me! We can't sleep here! Harold! You have to get us a room for the night. I demand it, I am certainly entitled to having a place to stay!"

Harold pointed at the crash site. "I am entitled to a new jet to fly us out of here. But I don't think I am going to get one!"

Alexandria got mad. "Stupid cis white male and your stupid white-supremacist-cis-hetero-patriarchal-capitalist culture! Thinking beyond your western ideologies requires that I embrace different ways of communicating as an anti-racist feminist!" She smiled smugly as she pressed the SOS button on her cell phone screen. But as she waited, her smug superior smile, slowly turned upside down, as nothing happened. She started pressing the button again and again, faster and faster. "Why isn't this working!" She sobbed. Out of frustration she leaned back her head and screamed loudly for a long time. Tired out, she looked at Harold and smugly said. "Someone will have heard that and come to our rescue."

Harold removing his fingers from his ears replied. "Impressive my dear. But the bang from the jet blowing up, was much louder and the fire was a massive distress flare. Yet, no one came to put the fire out. No emergency response at all. Not so much as a single nosey neighbor telling us stop making so much noise."

Richard asked meekly, "Are we really alone, Dad?"

Harold looked sad, "Yes, it certainly appears to be the case. We will have to search the island to be sure. But for now, we need to bed down for the night."

Alexandria was still angry. "We can't sleep on the ground! This is oppression! It is discrimination!"

Harold looked at her and said, "This is reality. But we don't have to sleep on the ground. While we still have light, open your suitcases and see what we have to work with."

The Rocks opened their suitcases and Harold directed them in using some of their clothes to make a sort of sleeping mat for them to lay on, with a few large clothing pieces to use as a blanket. He also showed them how to roll up a piece of clothing to use as a pillow. Amelia pulled out a stuffed teddy bear and lay down between her parents. Richard lay down on the outside edge next to his father.

As they laid there watching the sky slowly growing darker, they shifted around trying to get comfortable on the uneven ground and bumpy clothing. Amelia asked, "Where are we going to go for breakfast in the morning?"

Harold signed. "A very good question. We will have to find out in the morning.

Chapter Five

Harold woke up early to discover the spectacular morning glory of a tropical island sunrise. He got up out of their makeshift bed and climbed over Richard. He stood up, climbed the sand dune, and looked out across the beach with rolling waves, back lit by the orange glow of the sun, just starting to break above the horizon. Richard stood next to him and said, "Wow, that is something."

Harold said, "Yes, it is, and not a single jet trail in the sky. Not only are we off the beaten path, we are way off. Captain Allah seems to have been an over achiever when it comes to screwing up and getting really lost."

"Any idea where we are Dad?"

"Our dear departed captain, flew for so long, and not necessarily in a straight line, we could be anywhere in the Pacific. And, I only say Pacific because otherwise we probably would have crashed on more than an island. But judging from the temperature and the palm trees, I would guess, somewhere in the south pacific."

Richard looked out at the long deep tracks made by the jet's wheels, which ran straight along the beach to the rocks blackened by yesterday's fire. "We really did crash on the rocks."

"Yes, we did, managed to hit the only rock in this entire section of beach. We had a very talented pilot to end up way out here in the middle of nowhere and succeeded in completely destroying our plane along with everything in it."

Amelia asked, "What about breakfast?"

Alexandria put her hand on her stomach. "I really need a bathroom. Have you found a bathroom yet Harold?"

Harold looked around and walked onto the beach and picked up a piece of metal from the plane. He found a rock and walked down to the blackened rock. He took the rock and pounded on the metal. He came back with the metal piece in his hand. "Here you go, I made a small shovel so you can dig a hole."

Alexandria was puzzled and looked at Harold like he was an idiot. She spoke slowly as if speaking to a child she was mad at. "Why do you think I would want to dig a hole? When what I want to do is to use a bathroom?"

Harold told her why and she gasped in horror. "I am never doing something so vile. Not ever. Now just find me a bathroom and be quick about it."

Harold shrugged. "This island doesn't seem to come equipped with bathroom faculties."

Alexandria pulled out her phone. "Not even a handicapped bathroom? I am going to report them. Desperate times calls for desperate actions, I will just have to search for the nearest Starbucks and hope there are not too many needles on the floor. Harold you really need to do better in picking out vacation spots. Next time I will pick."

Harold pointed out, "Dear, there are no Starbucks here."

Alexandria was getting frustrated with her phone. "Oh, don't be stupid. There is always a Starbucks nearby. I should have thought of this last night." After a few minutes of failing to even get a signal she said, "Alright, we will have to go look for one."

Richard asked, "Just how does this hole thing work?"

Harold smiled, "Here I will give you a demonstration."

Amelia said, "I coming too!"

Harold awkwardly said, "This trip is for the boys, next one is for the girls."

Amelia pointed out, "But you are taking Prissy and she is a woman. I am non-binary, so it doesn't matter."

Harold looked like he had just been hit by the semi-truck of reality. After a long pause, he tried talking, hoping his brain could catch up to his mouth. "Ah, um, well you see, this trip is for people with penises and the second trip will be for people with vaginas."

Amelia looked thoughtful. "Oh, why is that?"

Harold heard the dreaded 'why' and being a parent, knew he was in trouble. Trying not to dig the hole any deeper, metaphorically of course, he replied. "It is customary in most societies that people with penises and vaginas, use separate bathrooms for reasons of modesty and decency. It is why people wear clothes, we don't want to be seen nude and certainly not by someone of the opposite sex when using the bathroom."

Amelia was confused, "Then why does Prissy use the woman's bathroom if she has a penis?"

Harold was now confused as he had unintentionally boxed himself in. He felt like Houdini, trying to escape from a safe he had just locked himself in. Richard tried to come to his rescue. "I use a woman's bathroom because I am a transwoman. I am a woman trapped in a man's body. I identify as a woman, so I am a woman."

Amelia simply stated the obvious. "You have a penis. You should use the bathroom for people with penises. The woman's bathroom is for people with vaginas. Like Dad said, the vagina people don't want you in their bathroom."

Richard got angry. "I have rights! I have the right to use the bathroom I identify with!"

Amelia feeling a bit cocky with her new knowledge was reveling in the power of its simple logic her big brother couldn't see. "Don't the people with vaginas have a right to their own bathroom?"

Richard madly stated, "I have a right and I am entitled to be a woman and a woman's bathroom."

Amelia pointed out, "But by exercising your right, you take away theirs by invading their privacy. The very reason why Dad said there are two different bathrooms."

Richard was frustrated by his little sister's logic and said, "I am a woman!"

Amelia having successfully connected the dots, said, "I am more of a woman than you will ever be Richard. Because I actually am, what you pretend to be. Someday I will have a baby and nurse it. I will be its mother. Because that is what women are made to do, we are built for it. You just don't have the right equipment for it, brother. I always said you needed a shrink. You need to face the fact that you are a man. You have to learn to be like Dad, not Mom. You are going to be a daddy, not a mommy, someday, so you had better start getting ready for the job."

Richard screamed and charged at his sister. Harold blocked his son and pushed him back, causing him to fall on his back. Richard curled into a fetal position and sobbed, repeating over and over again. "I am a woman!"

Harold turned to face Amelia and sternly told her. "Apologize to Prissy and tell her, she is a woman."

Amelia put her hands on her hips. "No, that would be a lie. Richard needs to deal with reality. He is a man. He has to see that and deal with it."

Alexandria decided to correct her daughter. "Pandora, I would think a non-binary person like yourself would be more sympathetic to a transgender woman like your sister."

Amelia took a step back and after moment of thought said, "I am a woman, or at least a girl. Because I have a vagina. I am not non-binary. I only said that because everyone kept pushing all this crazy sexual stuff on me. I'm only 14, mother, and you let them come after me with all this perverted adult stuff I wasn't ready to deal with. I didn't even know what all the trans this and that even meant. I was only a kid. I needed you to help me to become a woman, not tell me I am something weird so you can score social points with your friends. All I ever wanted was for you to be my MOM!" Amelia broke down and cried.

Alexandria was horrified. "I am so sorry baby. I didn't mean for it to be this way. I will always be your mom and you will always be my little girl." She put her arms around her daughter and hugged her. Amelia stopped crying and hugged her back. "Thanks Mom."

Harold watched this drama unfold not sure what to do. He looked at his son crying on the ground. He walked over to Richard and went down on one knee and put his hand on his son's shoulder. "I think I am beginning to see I may have made some mistakes which made life harder for you. I will always be your father and you will always be my son."

Richard rolled over quickly and jumped to his feet and raised his fists ready to fight. "I am a woman, Dad! I am your daughter, not your son!" He turned to face his little sister. Harold stepped in front of him and raised his arms like a football blocker. Richard called out over Harold's shoulder at Amelia, loudly shouting, and pointing at her, "You are transphobic! You are trying to oppress me by misgendering me, that is a crime! I am reporting this to . . . to . . . somebody!"

Amelia shouted back, "Who are you shouting to Richard? There is no one here to hear us. It is just us. Nobody cares because nobody is here. You are dependent on a norm of a society that doesn't exist here. You are a fish out of water, a trans out of San Fransico, you are out of your element. There is no one rushing to defend your entitlement to something that is not yours."

Alexandria stood up and said, "Pandora, that is no way to speak to your sister, apologize at once!"

Amelia, stopped and said, "I apologize for how I said it, but not for what I said."

Alexandria glared at Amelia and walked over to Richard. "Come with me to Starbucks and you can use the bathroom with me."

Richard awkwardly said, "You're my mother, I don't want to use a bathroom with you."

Alexandria was stunned. "What! We are both women. You are my daughter. Why wouldn't you use a bathroom with me?"

Richard squirmed. "Mom! I am too old to use a bathroom with my mother."

Alexandria was surprised by this turn of events. "Well, if it makes you feel uncomfortable. But come, let's go find a bathroom."

The four of them walked into the jungle to look for a Starbucks. Harold took his shovel along.

After walking for a while without finding a Starbucks, Harold said, "I'm going to do my business, I will be right back." As he gestured with the shovel.

Richard raised his hand. "I'll go too."

Alexandria looked sternly at him. "Prissy! I thought you were going to wait until we get to Starbucks."

Richard was stepping around impatiently. "I have to go now Mom."

"Oh, alright then."

Once they came back, they continued on. After about an hour, Alexandria exasperatedly said, "I can't make it to Starbucks. I think I am going to wet my pants."

Amelia cheerfully spoke up. "I know what to do. Follow me, Mom!" She took the shovel from Harold and headed off into the jungle. Alexandria meekly followed behind her. A few minutes later they came back. Alexandria was much more relaxed and said, "That wasn't so bad. But I still need a coffee and some breakfast at Starbucks."

After they walked on more, Harold suddenly turned and hurried forward. He stopped and pointed. "I found your Starbucks."

"Where! Where! I hope they have avocado toast!" Alexandria said excitedly as she hurried towards Harold. "Where is it?" She asked him.

He pointed at the large puddle of water. "Right there, our island Starbucks." He then got down on his belly and put his mouth down in the water and drank deeply. "Ah, this is great water."

Alexandria asked, "What do you think you are doing? Drinking dirty water out of a puddle!"

The kids followed his example and filled up on the water. Alexandria yelled. "Stop them! Stop them, Harold! That water is polluted!"

Harold said, "Hopefully not. But it is all we have. I think it's a spring, so it should be pretty clean. We will have to see if any of us get sick from it, then we would have to try and find a better source of water."

"Harold, I am not drinking that water. I want coffee at Starbucks." With that, Alexandria started walking. They followed her through the jungle until Harold said, "look, fruit." He went to the tree and picked some and pealed one and took a bit. "Mango, I think. Looks like there are some other fruits on those trees over there."

He picked another and handed it to Alexandria. She looked it over and peeled it. She gingerly took a bit and chewed. Then she tore into it.

A while later they all sat on the ground relaxing after breakfast. Harold asked Alexandria, "Do you still want to go looking for Starbucks?"

She threw a mango peel away and said sadly, "No, I give up."

Harold said, "We have found water and food. Now we need to find shelter. We want a roof over our heads before it rains."

Alexandria asked, "What are we going to do?"

Harold smiled, "You are going to love it. We are going house shopping. But our first house here will be a small fixer upper. We will have to look around for a good spot, to build a shelter, near food and water."

Richard pointed out, "This looks like a good place."

Harold pointed his finger like a teacher making a point, "We need to think about materials. We can't cut down these trees here, or there would be no food near us. We need to look for things to build with, near where we want to live."

It took them the rest of the day to use the makeshift shovel as a makeshift saw to cut enough palm branches, to make a crude thatched shelter over some large branches that served as rafters. They followed the trail they had made when they walked into the jungle, to go back and pack their suitcases. On the way back to the shelter, Alexandria was tired. Richard took her suitcase and carried it for her. "Thank you, Prissy. It is good you are so strong."

Richard asked his mom, "Isn't being strong a guy thing?"

Alexandria was tired. "Women are just as strong as men."

"But mother, why am I carrying your stuff, instead of you carrying mine? I am stronger than all the other women in swim class. I think it is because I used to be a man."

"Well, yes, but women can be just as strong as men."

Richard replied. "Maybe, but certainly not on average, or I would not be stronger than all other women in my class and in the other schools we swim against. I mean I am not just a little bit stronger. I blow them out of the water. They don't have much of a chance against me. Unless Wonder Woman shows up someday, I got them all beat. And that is because I used to be a man. That is why I think strength is a man's thing and not a woman's. It sort of makes me uncomfortable being strong, being a woman."

Alexandria was hanging on to his elbow as he walked. "Well don't give up being strong. We really need your strength. We never would have got the shelter built without your strength."

Over the next few days, they developed a routine of gathering fruit, improving their shelter, and looking for things they could use. Harold announced, "We need to explore the island to see what else is here we could use. I was thinking to take Prissy with me, while you two stay near the shelter."

Amelia excitedly said, "I want to go too."

Harold had been expecting this. "I think this trip will be a bit dangerous. I want to climb the peak to see the whole island. I don't know how difficult the climb will be. But it could save a lot of time in finding out what is here."

Richard spoke up, "Shouldn't I stay here with the rest of the women?"

Richard had a sad look for a moment. "The climb could be very dangerous. If I fell and got hurt, I could die. It would be much safer to have someone strong with me. Together, we would be stronger and safer than one alone."

They all agreed it would be the safest way.

Chapter Six

The next morning Harold and Richard set out after breakfast and walked through the jungle toward the central peak of the island. Harold was wearing the same clothes he had worn on the plane, washed in water and air dried, practical tropical jungle pants and a long sleeve shirt. He had also pulled out his sun hat from the suitcase. Richard wore a woman's bright pink exercise sweats and pink running shoes. Together they hiked through the brush. Harold cut a large leaf off now and then, dropping it on the center of their trail, to help guide them back.

The jungle turned steeper and rockier as the approached the peak. It became more and more rock climbing as they stepped from one large rock to another. The trees thinned out, as there were less places for soil to collect or for a root to grow. Soon, they cleared the tree line. They stopped and looked around. Behind them, over the jungle below them, was nothing but the ocean stretching as far as they could see. They resumed climbing. The peak turned into a near vertical wall of volcanic rock. Not strong enough to be trusted, they worked round it. Until they found a pathway, worn by water, which ran up to the top of the peak. They climbed it to the very top. Harold stood on the peak while slowly turning and looked all around. "It is an island, and a fairly small one."

Richard pointed, "I see two more islands over there."

Harold looked and asked, "Where? I don't see them."

Richard pointed his arm very straight, "There and there."

"Good eyes . . . Prissy. Looks like they are very far away, miles away. Nothing we could swim to."

Richard looked hard trying to measure the distance with his eyes. "I don't know. I am a very good swimmer, even compared to men. But it would be very hard and dangerous if I could even do it. I don't know how I could stay on course, since down in the water, I would not be able to see them."

His father said, "And there would be sharks. Plus, once you got there, there might be nothing there and you would have to swim back, all for nothing."

His son thought it over, "I agree, too dangerous. Unless we could make it safer somehow."

Harold reasoned, "The thing which matters is, if there is anyone over there who can help us. It is possible they didn't see the smoke from the jet crash because of this peak. But maybe they would notice a signal fire here or on the beach."

Richard said, "It would probably have to be here. The beach is below their horizon. They would only be able to see the smoke after it had spread out. But from here, it is a direct line of sight. At night they could see the fire light directly."

Harold agreed, "I think you are on to something. Before we head down, let's see if we can see anything interesting on the island from here."

Richard asked, "What is that white line? It runs around the island offshore."

Harold said, "That's the reef. If you look over there, there is a gap in the reef and a bay or harbor down there. Too far to go today. It is on the far side from us."

After they had seen all that where was to see, Harold said, "Let's head back."

Once they got back to the shelter, they discovered Alexandria crying as she mourned the first death of their party. "She's dead! I tried everything, but it is no use. She is dead. How can I go on? How can I live without her?"

Harold and Richard were stunned. Harold asked, "Where is she?"

Alexandria sobbed as she pointed to the shelter. Harold rushed in but didn't see Amelia anywhere. He rushed back out and hurriedly asked Alexandria, "Where is Amelia?"

Alexandria between deep sobs, gasped out, "How would I know?"

"Hi, Dad, I am right over here." Amelia said as she walked out of the bush carrying some fruit.

Harold was confused. "Mom said you were dead."

Alexandria cried out, "Not her, my cellphone!"

Amelia explained, "Her cellphone battery died."

Harold said, "Oh. Well, Alexandria, if you wanted to get the news, Richard and I have some for you."

She stopped weeping. "What?"

Harold stated, "We are indeed on an island. But there are two other islands we can see, but they are far away. There is also a reef around the island and a harbor on the other side."

Alexandria thought she saw light at the end of the long dark tunnel. "We have to go there right now, so I can recharge my phone at a Starbucks!"

Richard put his hands up. "Wait Mom! Dad meant harbor in the sense of a ship could go there, not that there were any. All we saw on the other side of the island was jungle."

Harold tried to calm her down. "In a few days, Prissy and I will go over there and check it out."

Amelia held up a rope. "Look what Mom showed me how to make."

Harold looked at the crude rope. "How did you make this?"

Amelia smiled, "Mom showed me how to braid the palm leaves."

Harold was excited. "This is great. We could use rope to make a better shelter. We could tie down the palm leaves, so they don't blow off. We could make baskets for carrying. If you can braid, maybe you can weave things like sleeping mats or even clothes."

Amelia's face lit up. "Mom, did you hear that? Can you show me how to do that?

"Sure dear, just look for a video on YouTube . . ." Alexandria broke off and sobbed again, "my phone, my phone."

Over the next few days, Harold picked up pieces of metal from the plane and made knives of various sizes and shapes. Alexandria taught Amelia braiding and hand weaving. Together they made ropes which got better as they worked at it. Harold used some rope to fasten a large knife to a long pole like branch to use as a spear. The girls used the small knives he made to cut fruit and fibers for braiding and weaving. Harold next took a long branch and cut one end to a point. He used a rock to pound it into the ground. The end sticking up, he cut into another point. He grabbed a coconut and impaled it on the sharp stick and twisted to split the husk. After a few tries, he learned how to husk coconuts. After knocking a hole in one end, they had their first coconut milk, which fast became a family favorite. The coconut meat was a welcome addition to their diet.

As they were finishing lunch, Harold holding up a piece of coconut meat, said, "What is really needs is to be toasted. It would taste so much better that way."

Alexandria said, "Light the stove and I'll toast some up for you." She smiled.

Harold thought about it and said, "About time we did just that. We can cut firewood and build a campfire ring with some stones. But we don't have a way of lighting a fire."

Richard asked, "Don't we have any matches?"

Harold shook his head, "Nope, going to have to do it the old way."

The next morning Harold took Richard with him. They cut the driest wood they could find, gathered stones and made a campfire ring. Harold got down to business. "They taught us this in survival class, but I have never done it myself."

His family watched as he rubbed a pointed stick in a grooved piece of wood. He rubbed it back and forth, trying to get it hot. Next, he crushed up some very dried leaves and sprinkled some in the groove. He rubbed the hot point of the stick faster in the groove until there was a hint of smoke. He stopped and gently blew until a small fire appeared. He quickly fed it the edge of a dry leaf. It lit, and he touched it to a small pile of dried leaves which started to burn. He carefully added small pieces of wood until he had a campfire burning.

Harold leaned back and caught his breath away from the smoke. As his family cheered and clapped. Harold tiredly said, "I can't believe it worked on the first try."

Richard said, "Dad, you worked on it all afternoon."

Alexandria with Amelia helping, toasted coconut which they all enjoyed. As the sun went down, they talked around the fire, before letting it burn out and going to bed.

Chapter Seven

It was another beautiful sunrise in paradise, as Harold and Richard headed back to the crash site. Harold had his spear and Richard had a rope. They made their way over the blackened rock, to the water's edge. Harold stood and looked into the water. Once he spotted a fish, he waited until it came close, and he speared it. The fish twisted trying to get off the spear, but the barbs held it. Harold lifted it out of the water and showed Richard how to put the rope through the gills to hold it.

"Dad, why are you spear fishing?" Richard asked.

Harold spoke as a matter of fact, "For food of course."

"But Dad, I am a vegan!" Richard said angrily.

"Past tense, Prissy. Not a lot of protein choices here. Humans require protein in their diet." Harold pointed out in a voice of reason.

"You are going to force me to eat meat?" Richard said in a high enough voice, that he almost sounded like a woman.

"No of course not. Circumstances will do that." Harold simply.

"What do you mean?" He asked worriedly.

"I think you will find out, when we cook this." Harold said with a smile.

Before they had left camp that morning, Harold had dug in the hot ashes, and placed some small pieces of wood and covered them with ash. When they returned, he dug them out and let the air hit the hot blackened wood. After one gentle breath, a flame appeared. Harold put on more wood and got the fire going. Once they had a good bed of coals, he used the flat homemade pan they had used for the coconut. He put the cleaned fish in the pan and slowly heated it over the coals. The fish had enough fat on them to fry well.

Richard had watched all of this with disgust. "I can't believe you are actually going to eat that. How would you like it if some fish took a bite out of you and ate you!" He said with entirely too much emotion for a fish story.

Harold didn't even look up. "They are called sharks. Eat or be eaten. That is what survival is all about. Do you want to be the predator or the prey?"

Richard was disgusted by all of this. "Neither we should all just get along."

Harold looked back over his shoulder at his confused son. "Try that with a hungry shark. We don't have a choice. We need protein. Our sources for it are limited. I can't exactly run off to Whole Foods and pick up a soy burger for you."

Richard was trying to think of come back, when he was hit by the aroma of frying fish. He felt a sudden twist in his stomach and heard it growl.

Harold smiled, "Ah the roar of the predator when it smells food."

Richard was shocked by his body's reaction. He tried to fire off a quick response but had to pause to wipe his mouth. He was drooling, his mouth was watering.

Alexandria and Amelia came out of the brush. Alexandria purred. "That smells just heavenly, Harold."

The girls quickly got set up for lunch. Harold served the fish hot from the pan onto their wooden plates. They ate with homemade knives and chop-sticks which had been made exactly the way it sounded. Richard refused to take any fish, until Harold said, "Just try a small piece to see if you like it."

Richard accepted a small piece of hot fish, picked it up with the chopsticks and dropped it into his mouth. That was when the magic happened. It was the best thing he had ever tasted in his life. It seemed like every fiber in his body was begging for more. "I guess I could eat just a little more."

Harold smiled and put a large piece on his plate. Harold said, "Not so fast, there is plenty more and watch out for the fish bones." As Richard tore into the fish.

Later as they sat round the fire, Amelia said enthusiastically, "That was the best fish ever Dad!"

Harold laughed. "It is true, because hunger is the best cook. We just really needed the protein."

One morning a few days later, Harold and Richard set out to hike to the far side of the island. Too shorten the distance, they hiked towards the peak, until the jungle thinned. They then walked around the base of the peak, to reach the other side of the island. They talked as they walked. Richard again wearing his pink woman's exercise suit, asked, "Why do you always take me on these hikes Dad?"

Harold looked back over his shoulder. "Do you think Pandora or your mother could do this kind of hiking? What if I fell and got hurt? Would they have the strength to help me back to camp?"

"Dad, you keep treating me like a man, because of my strength. You are discriminating against me."

Harold smiled. "You know, a month ago, I would have agreed with you. But now, here on this island, I see things differently. Do you know why? It's because we must face reality. I have been forced by our circumstances to rethink how I see things. I mean, if you were to drop a whole pile of hundred-dollar bills in front of me, I would probably use them to start a fire."

Richard was puzzled. "Because you already have so much money?"

"No, because here money has no value. The most important thing in my life is now worthless. I spent all my life ignoring the really important things in life while I wasted my life on things which actually have little value in the bigger picture."

Richard was intrigued by this sudden change in his billionaire father. "What could be more important than your wealth, father?"

Harold stopped and turned to look at his son and pointed at him. "You are. You, Alexandria, and Pandora are the most important things in my life. It took getting plane crashed on a remote island to pound it into my thick head. That the people I love are more important than money."

Richard was puzzled. "You love me?"

Harold looked at his son. "Since the day you were born. I guess I haven't been very good about showing it. I am sorry I haven't been a very good father to you."

Tears came to Richard's eyes as he rushed forward and embraced this father and cried on his shoulder. After a while, He said, "I love you too Dad." In a shaky voice.

Harold patted his son on his back. "It is alright. We have both been through some hard times here which have made us rethink our lives."

Richard stepped back and wiped the tears from his eyes. "Thanks Dad."

They started hiking again, but Harold stopped and pointed. He said with increasing excitement. "Look! An old trail! See how it is cut into the side of the peak. I bet it goes all the way to the top. We were probably on part of it when we were up there and didn't know it! The other end probably goes where we want to go!"

With that, Harold turned and started walking down the old trail into the jungle. Richard asked worriedly, "Do you think we will run into people? Maybe headhunters or cannibals?"

Harold in a good mood laughed. "You have seen too many old movies. They probably all have cell phones now and eat soy burgers." Harold's mood soured a bit. "I don't think we will find anyone. This trail is too overgrown. It looks like it hasn't been used in a very long time."

As they walked downhill through the jungle, Harold pointed, "Look it's a black stone wall, like they have in Hawaii."

Soon there was a black rock wall on each side of the trail. Harold said, "I think we're in an old village."

Richard pointed to their right. "Looks like there's a building over there."

They turned off the trail and forced their way through the thick jungle undergrowth to black wall of stone. Harold pointed, "Stairs" they climbed the short stairs and found themselves standing on a large rectangular platform.

Richard asked, "What is it?"

Harold stood with his hands on his hips as he slowly turned around surveying everything in sight. "House foundation. See the holes for wall posts. This is really a great piece of real estate, look at the views. Must have been the chief's house."

Harold walked quickly back towards the steps with purpose in his stride. "Come on, let's check out the neighborhood!"

He got back to the trail and followed it down through the jungle past several other smaller rock foundations until it opened up. There before them, was a white sandy beach surrounding the harbor bay they had seen from the top of the peak. Harold pointed out at the sea. "There is the opening in the reef. You can almost see where they must have pulled the dugout canoes up on the beach over there."

They spent a few hours exploring the old village before deciding to head back. Harold said, "We should head back, but I am thinking we should try walking back on the beach."

Richard asked, "Why?" It will take longer."

"Yes, it will, but we haven't gone that way yet. More opportunity to explore and find things. It may be a much easier walk."

"We would get back quicker the other way."

"I want to check it out to see if the beach route would be easier for your mother and sister. I am thinking we should move here."

"Why Dad? We are just getting set up at our camp."

"Yes, we are. But the people who once lived here picked this site as the best place to live for a reason. We found their freshwater source. The bay is fantastic, and they have a cut trail to the peak. I think we will find a lot of things they did that could turn out to be very useful."

"A case of why reinvent the wheel?"

Harold smiled excitedly, "Exactly! They have already done the hard work for us. We just have to figure out how to use it."

They started walking back along the beach. Richard asked, "But Dad, isn't this cultural appropriation?"

Harold shook his head, "We still have a lot to talk about."

Several hours later, Harold said, "You see how it can't possibly be colonialist exploitation and oppression of the island culture, when they are all dead and long gone. How oppressed can a dead person feel?"

Richard argued back, "But we do not know or understand their culture. We may be violating their taboos. They could have found our presence here very offensive."

Harold said, "The problem here is you have a problem. The dead people don't have a problem with any of this, because they are dead. The actual cultural appropriation here, is you, trying to imagine objections a culture you know nothing about, may or may not have had."

"But we are white colonist oppressors taking over their village and land."

Harold smiled, "They are welcome to deport us back to the mainland."

"Dad, this is not a joke. It is a very real problem of cultural appropriation offending minority cultures."

Harold kept walking as he said, "I used to read about this all the time. Young white activists defending and suing to protect a group from their culture being appropriated. But the minority group, often likes it and embraces it since it increases interest in their culture and increase sales of their artwork and crafts."

"It is still wrong, just because some members of a culture sell out for profit, that doesn't make it right. Even if even just one member is offended, it is wrong."

Harold scoffed. "If even just one person was offended? If that was the standard for everything, nothing could ever happen. It is impossible to please everyone. You can't let the objections of a few, stop everything. The world would grind to a halt, and everyone would starve."

"Surely you are exaggerating."

"Well, maybe not. We have an excellent example right here. You object to our moving into the old village as cultural appropriation. Now if because of that, we decide not to, we could end up staving due to having less access to food and material sources."

"Dad, you are exaggerating!"

"I wish I was. I don't want to worry you. But we are in a life and death survival situation. Our lives hang in the balance. Our very survival depends on us making the best choices to survive. Moving into the village appears to be our best choice. To do otherwise, would reduce our chances of survival."

Richard's face went through a series of contortions as his logic and feelings battled each other. After a while he said, "You are right Dad. I still don't like it though."

Harold laughed. "If my family was freezing, I would roll up the Constitution and use it to light the Mona Lisa, to keep them alive."

Chapter Eight

Alexandria was excited but worried about the move. "Harold, is it a better neighborhood? Did the former villagers have equal rights for LGBTQIA+ people and reproductive rights equal access to medical care for women?"

Harold was quite taken aback and didn't know how to answer. "They are all dead and gone for a long time. I have no idea."

Alexandria was quite firm. "I don't want to move into a far-right neighborhood where rights would not be respected."

"Dear, they are all dead."

"But did you see any Trump signs or American flags?"

Harold thought this was crazy, which puzzled him since a month ago he would have asked the same questions. "Not so much as a Post Office flagpole. Not a single Trump sign or American flag anywhere and it is the west coast of the island."

She smiled, "Sounds like a great place to live. Let's move. Are you going to hire or just rent a U-Haul?"

Harold smiled until he realized she was serious. "Nobody to rent from, we will have to do it ourselves."

"You checked in the village?"

Yes, dear, not so much as a hand cart. We will have to move our stuff ourselves."

Alexandria did not like the sound of that. "That's impossible. We have too many things to carry them to the other side of the island!"

Harold calmly explained, "We do it in steps, and only take with us, what we need. We don't need to bring things which are already there. Like palm branches or firewood. Prissy and I will go first and build a new shelter. Then we will carry some of our things over there and put them in the shelter. Last, we all go over together taking along the last of our things."

After a few days restocking fish and fruits, Harold and Richard were on the beach, hiking back to the village. They each wore a handmade backpack, filled with metal tools, lots of rope and dried fish, along with some of their dishes and things. Richard adjusted his heavy pack, "I thought a minimalist lifestyle backpack would be a lot lighter."

Harold laughed. "Minimalism works for backpacking but not for a lifestyle."

Richard asked, "Why not?"

"Human nature, we collect things. We are by nature hoarders. It is engrained in our genes to store stuff for the future. For the coming winter, the next hard times. Many people learned that hard lesson in the Great Depression."

"But aren't people happier with less things?"

"Less to worry about, sure. But some are happier if they feel prepared. Look at us, we could have stayed on the beach living literally out of our suitcases. But instead, we built a shelter and are moving to a better place to live. Minimalism is fine, but you should always have a backup plan and be prepared for the future. What if a rainstorm had caught us while we were still living on the beach? We could have died of hypothermia or exposure."

Richard thought about this and said, "But, Dad, aren't you a hypocrite? Since you own so many things we don't need?"

"Good point. But there is a deference between owning what you can afford and owning what you can't afford, especially if you do it on credit. But I have been rethinking my life and some of the choices I have made. Maybe we would be better off with a lot less. Look at how happy we are now with almost nothing."

Richard was puzzled for a moment. "You know, I would not have believed it, but you are right. I feel much happier now being on this island, then I did back home. Why is that?"

Harold put his hand on his son's shoulder. "I am very glad to hear that. If you think about it, in time you will figure it out and see how in some ways we are better off here."

Richard asked, "What would you have done differently?"

Harold took his hand back and gestured. "Spend more time with family. Cut back on time at work. Maybe even work remotely most of the time. Yes, buy less stuff. The jet was obviously a mistake. I don't regret the armored car one bit. One of my best investments."

Richard smiled. "Can't argue with you on that one. I am still amazed by what you did."

Harold looked around and said, "Truthfully, I screwed up. We only had to go through all that because I waited too long to get out. I am not talking about hours. I am talking about years. The handwriting had been on the wall a long time for San Fransico. I should have heeded it and left a long time ago. I shouldn't have waited until we needed a bullet proof car to get out alive."

Richard asked apprehensively, "What went wrong?"

Harold sadly said, "I think maybe some of the things we thought were good, turned out to be bad. We have been fed lies for so long, we have forgotten what truth is." He waved his hand around. "We have forgotten this is the real world and we have forgotten our role in it."

Richard was interested. "What role?"

"To survive, help others to survive. To take care of the earth, be good people and help others to be good people."

"But what is a good person?"

Harold laughed again. "I am still working that one out myself. But at least I am making progress. Back in San Fransico, it is a complete mystery or worst, a complete lie. I have seen the 'good people' of San Fransico do very evil things."

Richard asked, "What do you think, makes a good person?"

Harold rubbed his growing beard. "Well, you must face reality like this island has forced us to do, rather than live in a made up lie like we did in San Fransico. I think you need to have actual morals, rules to live by, that are real like this world. Not something based on the current direction the wind is blowing in the political world."

Richard was thoughtful and worried a bit at the same time. "What kind of morals are you talking about?"

Harold threw his hands up. "This is the part I am still working on. But the more I think about, I think traditional morals were traditional for a reason."

Richard was worried. "And what was the reason?"

Harold put his hands in his pockets. "They worked. They held society together and protected the family unit so there could be a next generation."

Richard exploded. "Dad, those people would have burned a transgender woman like me, at the stake!"

Harold looked over at his son. "Some of them may have. But that doesn't make it right. To disapprove of something is one thing, but to kill, is another. I don't agree with violence. We should obviously respect other people's opinions even if we don't agree with them."

Richard was nearly panicking. "What about me? Are you going to burn me at the stake?"

Harold stopped walking and turned to his son. "Of course not. I will always love you and protect you. Even if you think you're a woman."

Richard got mad. "Dad, I am a woman!"

Harold said, "Maybe you should look up the definition of what a transgender woman is."

"I know what it is, I AM A WOMAN."

Harold said very calmly. "Then why do you have to shout it?"

Richard decided his father was losing his marbles.

They reached the village and went to their future house. Together they cleared brush from around the foundation, cut palm fronds and set them aside for the roof. They also cut down small trees for their new shelter, set up a firepit and built a fire. In the evening they ate some of the food they had brought with them and slept on the pile of palm leaves.

In the morning after a quick breakfast, they got back to work, using the rope to tie branches together to create a frame for their shelter. Next, they tied rows of bundles of palm fronds in horizonal rows on the edges of the roof and row after row until they reached the top, which was finished with a thick folded row. The side walls were also covered except for the door. They restarted the fire. As they ate that night, Richard asked his dad, "I was thinking about what you said, and the reason why I have to shout, is because you don't believe me."

Harold said, "Shouting is an emotional response, not a rational one. It is not a counter argument, at least not a logical one."

Richard was exasperated, "What is it with you and being logical?"

Harold gestured around with his hands. "This is the real world. What is real is logical in that it exists. Things that are not logical, or can't be proven, do not exist because they are not real."

Richard stared. "You read that in a book!"

"Well maybe I am just an old boomer, who isn't always up on the latest thing. But are books bad now?"

Richard stared at his dad. "How can you not know most books are patriarchal propaganda! They preach the fantasy of patriarchal hegemony. The false racially oppressive belief the world needs white cis men to run it."

Harold smiled at this son. "I guess that makes history bad too."

Richard was puzzled. "Why do you say that?"

"Because history is real, and it is a record of both kings and queens. Kind of shoots a hole in hegemony thingy. Both the kings and queens messed up and created a lot of interesting times you didn't want to live in. Why most of the leaders were men, is simple, look at us now. Simple biology, why we are the ones doing this instead of your mother and sister."

Richard was shocked, "That is incredibly sexist. Woman can do everything a man can do."

Harold was still smiling. "Most things, but can they do them as well? If they were here instead of us, could they have done all the things we did today?

Richard was taken a back, "Humm, no they couldn't have. But two young college age women could have."

Harold turned over his right palm. "College women? Maybe highly trained athletes, perhaps swimmers? Now when you were on the men's team you were what, perhaps, average. But on the woman's team, you dominated."

Richard smiled, "I sure did. Oops, I guess I see your point. You see men's domination of women as mostly due to superior strength rather than some kind of male conspiracy against women?"

Harold's smile widened. "Yes, men tend to be stronger, so they tend to take the lead in labor and planning. And that is why we are here on this side of the island rather than the girls."

Richard rubbed his growing beard. "I think I see your point about something being real. I can't argue against your example, since as you said it is real and logical. OK, forget about the whole patriarchal hegemony conspiracy theory. But what about me, being a woman trapped in a man's body."

Harold dropped his smile and looked concerned. "I don't know if you are ready to hear this, so maybe just think about what I am going to say for a while. We both agree with the reality of you having a man's body. We can see that. But what we can't see, is if you have a woman's brain."

Richard tensed up but tried to keep his cool. "Yes, we agree about my body being male. But I am definitely a woman."

Harold said, "I don't want to push you too far, but think about this. We can see you are male on the outside, but what makes a brain male or female? Isn't it the body it's in? Any sexual differences in the brain would be caused by the sex of the body it's in."

Richard had a tear in one eye. "But I am a woman, why would I think I was a woman if I was a man?"

Harold looked intently at Richard, "Survival. Just as we do what we must do to survive on this island, you did what you had to do to survive in our old world. You know white cis males are supposedly the source of all evil. That, put you at a survival disadvantage. While transgender persons are a favored class, a survival advantage. You were only an average male swimmer, but a fantastic female swimmer. Unconsciously, you recognized you had a far better chance of survival if you became a woman. Your mind recognizing the survival advantages, flipped your mental gender switch without you even realizing why or how it happened. Suddenly you were a woman."

Richard was surprised. "Dad, you should have been a shrink. But it doesn't change the fact that I am a woman."

Harold shook his head. "Truthfully, I didn't think it would. But like I said, think about it. Think about this too, in our old world it was bad to be a white male, but here, it is good. Look at what you and I have been able to do, and we are just getting started."

The next morning, they hiked back and found the girls weaving sleeping mats. Amelia was laughing. They both seemed to be in a good mood. Alexandra asked, "How is our new shelter coming a long?"

Harold proudly said, "Its finished. I was thinking, Prissy and I would carry over another load of stuff, and then maybe the next day we could all go."

Alexandra thought this over. "That is great news. But we are low on dried fish. We should probably restock, before we move, in case the fishing isn't as good over there."

Harold was surprised Alexandra was thinking so logically, but tried not to let it show. "Yes, you are right. We will go fishing today and start drying the fish. May take us a few days to get enough, depending on if the fish are biting."

Amelia smiled, "Yes! Fresh fish for dinner tonight."

Harold and Richard had a great time fishing and caught much more than they were expecting. They cleaned them and used the back packs to haul them back. It was a great dinner. They spent the next two days drying fish over a small fire.

Harold and Richard put two of the suitcases, loaded with clothes, in the backpacks and hiked over and dropped them off at the shelter. They hiked back later in the day.

Moving day arrived. They packed the last two suitcases into the backpacks and managed to put the rest of their things in as well. The girls had made two smaller backpacks in which they carried the dried fish and some fruit. They were all set to go as they stood in front of their first shelter on the island. Alexandra put her hand out and touched the shelter. "It is silly, but I am going to miss this, our first home, on the island."

Harold said, "I think we will all always remember it. It was the turning point for us, learning how to survive and live on the island." He took his wife's hand and started walking toward the beach. Their children followed behind them.

They walked along the white sandy beach with the impossibly blue ocean breaking on the reef offshore. A few seagulls flew overhead. They talked as they walked. Harold pointed out to sea. "The waves are bigger today. I think, I see some dark clouds on the horizon over there."

Richard stopped and looked where his father was pointing. "Yes, you are right, and the wind is coming from there."

Harold said, "We may be getting some rain today. Hopefully we will reach the new shelter before it starts."

They unconsciously picked up their pace a bit as the wind gradually increased and the dark clouds grew closer. Alexandra worriedly said, "I hope the dried fish doesn't get wet, that could ruin it."

They were most of the way there when the dark storm clouds reached the island. It was very impressive as the sky over the sea was dark black with flashes of lightning behind the clouds, while the sky over the island was sunny and blue. The wind picked up and the hot sunny tropical air suddenly seemed to chill as the shadow of the storm passed over them. The storm was coming ashore as large waves slammed into the reef, which sent smaller waves to break on the beach. Waves now surged up across the white sand, wetting it. They tried to stay above the incoming waves to keep their shoes from getting soaked. The dry sand higher on the beach they were walking on, began to be hit by large drops of failing water. Each giant raindrop hit the dry white sand like a stone, creating a small crater of wet sand. A polka dot pattern appeared on the sand and was rapidly adding more dark dots as the rain increased. At last, they reached the edge of the village. They turned off the beach and were on a stone paved pathway underneath the jungle cover. Which was temporally shielding them from the rain, until the leaves got wet enough for the water to drip to the ground. Looking out under the trees they saw the bay was filled with big waves hitting the beach and the rocks. Water sprayed up into the air each time a big wave hit the rocks. The wind blew the spray inland. The wind blew through the tropical jungle tearing leaves off which flew through the air. They hurried uphill on the path towards their shelter, next to the rock platform. Harold was guiding Alexandria by her hand as he led her to the shelter. "There it is!" They ran into the small clearing and raced into the shelter. Richard was close behind with Amelia.

Inside the shelter it was dark and smelled of freshly cut palm fronds. The thick thatched roof and walls blocked much of the noise of the storm, making it quieter. This gave the shelter a feeling of safety from the storm outside. Sitting down on stone seats, they looked out the open doorway as the storm raged outside. The heavens opened up and a wall of water descended. The wind blew it horizontally through the jungle. The leaves ripped off the trees made the horizontal rain look green, like the jungle was a giant blender. The wind whipped through and around like a lion throwing its head about looking for something to sink its teeth into. The lightning came ashore too, with a vengeance as it flashed and boomed. A nearby tree exploded as the powerful heat of the bolt turned the sap into steam, blowing the tree trunk apart. As the thundercloud passed over the island, the lightning pounded the inland peak with strike after strike. Until the thunderstorm seemed to have exhausted its fury. The wind stopped, and the rain now came down in a steady downpour.

They all relaxed as the fury of the storm was replaced by the relaxing sound of falling rain. Alexandra looked around and said, "I don't see any leaks. This is a much better shelter, Harold."

Harold replied. "The ropes you and Pandora made, made all the difference. We were able to tie everything down, so nothing blew off."

Alexandra looked outside, "Still could use a door and maybe some windows."

Chapter Nine

By morning the storm had passed, and the rain had ended. The sun came up gloriously as if to apologize for the storm. They got up and had a breakfast of dried fish with some of the fruit they had brought along. After breakfast, they started to look over their new neighborhood to see what damage the storm had done. The ground of course was very wet and muddy. They soon found the storm although destructive, had left them a bounty of freshly fallen coconuts, which they gathered up. While searching for the coconuts they discovered trees damaged or blown down by the winds. Harold said to Richard, "The storm did our lumberjacking for us. We can use this to build our house."

Harold got out his makeshift axe and saw. They started cutting lumber and firewood. It took the four of them to move some of the heaver pieces to the building site. The wood cutting went on for a few days while the girls made more rope and gathered more palm leaves.

The next day dawned beautifully. With the dried fish running low, it was time to go fishing again. The four of them went down to the bay and started exploring it. A dead shark had washed up on the beach and smelled terrible. Harold walked up to it and put his hand on it. "This shark's skin is like sandpaper."

Richard pointed out, "We got a house to build, sandpaper would be very handy I imagine."

Harold grinned, "Yes it would, but would it work? We will have to try and find out. If my knives can cut this tough old shark, and how does one tan sharkskin?

Richard said, "Must be a way, they do sell sharkskin boots and jackets."

Alexandria and Amelia had moved down to the rocks, at the end of the beach. Alexandria called out, "Come see what I found!"

The boys headed over toward them. Harold looked inquiringly at Alexandria and she pointed at one of the tidal ponds. Harold didn't see anything. "What?" He asked.

"Oysters!" Alexandra smiled with her teeth showing a hungry grin.

Lunch had been quite an affair. All you can eat fresh raw oysters, was like paradise on earth, after two months of dried fish and fruit. Nobody moved after lunch. It was mid-afternoon before they began to stir. Dinner it was agreed would just be some fruit, since they were all still stuffed from lunch. They did have a fire after dinner, since they had plenty of firewood to burn. As they were sitting around on their inherited stone chairs, talking, Richard pointed at the peak. "We should take some of this firewood up there for a beacon fire."

Harold looked up at the peak. "Yes, definitely. But we should build the house first. Before we start hauling wood up there, we need to check the condition of the trail. We may need to fix it up a bit, so we can safely carry firewood up there."

Alexandria asked, "Why do you want to make a fire up there?"

Richard pointed out to sea. "From the peak, we could see the two islands that are out there. You can't see them from down here, but up there you can. If we light a fire up there, anyone on those islands should be able to see it."

Harold added, "Of course, they would have to be there to see it. We don't know if anyone lives on those islands."

Alexandria was excited. "We should do this!"

Harold tried to calm her down. "We will. But it will take a lot of time to haul the firewood up there. We don't know if there is anyone over there to see it. Which is why we should build the house first. We could be heading into a rainy season. The natives built houses for a reason."

The next morning Harold and Richard looked over the stone platform and cleaned out the postholes. Using some of palm trees the storm had blown down, they cut them to the same length and fitted them into the postholes. Fitting involved cutting away wood from the end until it fit snuggly in the posthole. That took all day. The next day they started cutting and fitting the cross pieces, which was harder since it required more cutting. They also had to lift them into place to trim them. It took ropes and poles to do it. Everyone slept well that night. The next step was the cross pieces the rafters would be connected to. A week later they were all in place. They used rope to tie down the purlins which went cross the rafters, to which the thatch would be tied. The palm fronds they had gathered earlier and the many the storm had blown down, were used for the roof.

Harold and Richard sat on the roof peak with a leg on each side, as they tied the last of the ridge thatching, in place. Richard looked at the completed roof of the house they had just built, "You were right Dad about us just getting started."

Harold wiped the sweat from his brow, "Yes, we are building our own home. Quite an accomplishment which we never could have done in our old world. Like I was saying, we are much more useful here than there."

Richard looked around at the ocean, the jungle, and the peak. "This really is an amazing place."

The walls were thatched the same way, but they added a doorway and window openings. Each opening was covered with a wood frame with palm fronds tied to them, using ropes for hinges.

At long last the house was done. They moved in and had their first dinner in the house. They sat on stone chairs around a stone table. The door and windows were open, revealing a beautiful ocean sunset with orange clouds. After dinner Richard said, "Dad, I have been thinking a lot about what you said. You are right. I think I only thought I was a woman, because it was what our old world was pushing me to believe. I was so mixed up in a mixed-up world. But here, everything is so real and simple. The simple truth is I am a man in man's body. It is so obvious. It took me awhile to see it. Anything else is nonsense. I don't want to live a lie anymore. I am done with all the poison we left behind. I am what I have always been, even if I didn't always know it. I am your son Richard."

Harold had tears of happiness, "Welcome back Richard, it is good to have my son back again."

Alexandria felt like someone had pulled the rug out from under her, turning her whole world upside down. "But Prissy, I have always supported you being a woman. Don't you want to be a woman anymore?"

Richard explained patiently, "Mother, it is not a question of what a person wants to be, but what they are. A cat can't decide to be a dog, it will always be a cat no matter what. It's the same with me, no matter how much I thought I was a woman, I was always still a man. I was never happy trying to be something I couldn't be. It was always so frustrating to be such a ridiculous failure, a big guy in a dress. Honestly, I was mentally ill. Everyone encouraging me, was making it worst by pushing me on a self-destructive course. Dad is right about how toxic our old world was and how I was poisoned by it. It was only here on this island; I was able to detox with help from Dad. I am free now, free to be my real self. A man who has found himself and is content with being who he is."

Alexandria pleaded, "Prissy, please don't give up. You can still be a woman. There is hormone therapy and surgery. You could have a woman's body."

Richard was repelled, and struggled to reply, "I never even considered doing that. Probably because deep down, I always knew I would always be a man. Even if I had done all that, I would still have been a man. Just a surgically altered man, made up to look like a woman. A sad, sick and twisted joke. Just imagine, what a mess I would now be in, if I had done that. I would be a man trapped in a man's body, reshaped to look like a woman. Instead of just needing to get my head straight, I would need a surgeon to repair my damaged body to try to restore it to what it once was."

Alexandria was horrified, "No Prissy, you would be my daughter, a woman."

Richard grimly carried on in his war of logic, "No, mother, I could never be your daughter. Even with the best surgeons on the planet, I never could have conceived and given birth to your grandchild. Because I am your son, not your daughter. As my sister said, I am going to be a daddy someday, not a mommy, and I had better start getting ready for the job." He turned and smiled at Amelia who smiled back.

Alexandria stubbornly continued, "Someday medicine will advance, and transwomen will be able to have children. You just have to hang in there Prissy. You can be a mother someday, and there is always adoption."

Richard pointed out, "Just because science can do something, doesn't mean we should. Even if one day we can truly turn men in women, it would be stupid to do so, when all you have to change is the mind. People just need to get their heads on straight. Perhaps someday science will be able to turn people into animals, but should we? What if I wanted to be surgically altered to look like a dog? Would you want me to do that?"

Alexandria's face contorted as her emotions battled each other, "No, I would not . . . Richard. You are right. I guess I am still living in our old world. I am still trapped by social pressure of people we may never see again. What does it matter what they think? You and your father, make sense, good practical sense. I am finally starting to understand it and see it. I am going to have to rethink my whole life and how I see things."

Harold looked at her and smiled, "Welcome to my club dear. The Club of Clear Thinkers."

Alexandria smiled back, "Do we have a secret handshake?"

Harold laughed, "No, but we could come up with one."

Amelia shouted, "I have my big brother back! I have my mom and my dad, back too. All my problems are gone. Pandora's box is now empty! Now I am no longer Pandora, I am Amelia once again."

Alexandria tiredly said, "I always did like the name Amelia better than Pandora, or we would have named you that when you were born. Looks like I will have to change the tags on half the laundry now."

Harold smiled, "I think are a family again." There were happy faces all around the table.

Chapter Ten

The next morning Alexandria and Amelia went to get water. They took empty coconuts in the small backpacks and filled them by holding them underwater in the stream, until the air stopped bubbling out. Once they were done, Amilia said, "Let's find out where the water comes from."

Alexandria agreed. The two of them followed the stream uphill through the jungle by walking barefoot over the black smooth rocks in the stream. They followed the stream and came around a turn. Amelia cried out, "It's a lake!"

Alexandria corrected her, "Pond, or rather, I think we just found our swimming pool."

They stripped and took a swim. Alexandria floated on her back, "This is just wonderful, the water is so cool and refreshing."

Amelia stood on the rocks under the small waterfall and rinsed off her hair. They laid out on the rocks in the sun, to dry. "Better than a spa and free membership for residents." Alexandria said as she relaxed.

Amilia asked, "Do we have to tell the boys?"

Alexandria said laughingly, "Of course we do. Just not right away. Men can join too, after a few days, if they pass the admission test of being good to us."

Harold and Richard hiked up the jungle trail toward the peak. Harold had on his usual jungle outfit, while Richard still wore his pink woman's exercise outfit. Richard complained, "I really should have packed more clothes. I feel so stupid wearing pink."

Harold said, "Look on the bright side, at least now you are smart enough to know it." Harold laughed. "Don't worry. I think I can spare you a few things. I tend to over pack."

"That would be great Dad. I really want to get out of woman's clothes. They are such a reminder of how dumb and foolish I was."

"We all make mistakes Son. You learn from them, and you keep going, wiser for your troubles."

They were coming up out of the jungle and reached the point where they had discovered the trail on their first trip across the island. Harold looked up at the peak above them. "All new trail ahead of us now. Keep your eyes open. Don't know what we may find and watch your footing. Don't want either of us falling."

They had only hiked a short way when Richard pointed off to their left. "There is something over there, a shadow."

Harold looked, "The trail turns and heads towards it."

They followed the trail. As they came around some large boulders, they saw a small valley cut in the mountain. There in front of them, was a small pond that fed a stream running down to the jungle. Harold pointed, "This must be where our fresh water comes from."

Richard looked the other way, "Dad, over there. It's a cave."

Harold turned and saw the dark opening in the rock wall of the peak. "How do we get over there?" He said, but saw the trail went to the opening of the cave. They walked over to the entrance and paused as they waited for their eyes to adjust to the darkness. Harold cautioned, "Caves can be extremely dangerous. If we go in, we must be very careful."

Richard anxiously said, "Dad, we have to check it out."

Harold smiled, "Of course we will check it out. I was just trying to sound responsible. At heart, I am still as young as you, this is exciting. Let's explore it but be careful."

Together they entered the cave. Harold noticed, "The trail goes inside the cave, there must be something in here."

They walked into the cave which had been created by the hot lava that had made the island. A lava flow had cooled on the outside, but cracked, allowing the hot center to run out creating a lava tube cave with dark black walls.

Water flowed in a channel in the cave floor with the trail running next to it. The cave turned to the left and the trail crossed the stream by a stone bridge to the other bank. They came around the turn to a large room with a skylight. The sunlight entered through the hole in the cave ceiling, hitting the lake in the center of the room. The room was filled with the sound of falling water from the waterfall on the far cave wall. The waterfall poured into the cave lake. The impossibly clear water revealed the smooth black rock bottom of the pool. Richard pointed into the darkness off to the side of the pond. "There is something over there." He started quickly walking toward it. Harold followed him. In the dim light, they could make out what looked like stone chairs and benches. There were even what appeared to be the remains of woven sleeping mats. Richard asked, "What is this?"

Harold smiled, "I think we found the island storm cellar. This must be where they sheltered from big storms like hurricanes."

Richard said, "That was a pretty big storm we had when we moved to this side of the island."

Harold looked glum, "It was nothing compared to a hurricane. I am glad to find this, worried however, they needed one. We will have to keep an eye on the weather. This is a bit of a hike from the village, yet they somehow knew when they had to use it. They knew when the big storms were coming somehow."

After looking around for a while, they walked back out of the cave. Harold looked around outside the cave until he spotted where the trail broke off and went to the peak. "There is where the trail continues up the mountain."

They inspected the condition of the trail as they climbed towards the top. As the trail steepened, the trail turned into stone steps cut into the rock. The steps took them up much easier than climbing the other side had been. Harold pointed at the trail, "Here is here we joined the trail last time we climbed the peak."

At the top, they looked out over the whole island, and it seemed the whole ocean. Richard scanned the horizon and checked the distant islands. "Not a ship or plane in sight, at least not that I can see."

Harold was also looking hard. "Same here, not a thing."

Harold walked around on the peak and inspected it. "This looks like the best place for the beacon fire. Over there is where we would probably spend the night."

Richard was surprised, "What do you mean, spend the night?"

"Just think about it, we come here and wait until after sunset to light the fire. It would be too dark to take the trail down. Better we camp out up here and keep an eye on the fire and watch to see if anyone signals back."

"Good point Dad, forgot about when we would be lighting the fire. Couldn't we just light it earlier, leaving us enough time to get home before dark?"

"I thought about that. The problem is we would waste the brightest part of the fire before it was dark, and we will need to feed it to keep it going, rather than lighting off all the wood at once. We will have much more control if we are here."

Richard looked around, but he wasn't so sure about this, "Great view, the stars will be fantastic, but it looks like it will be windy and cold at night."

"Yes, we will need a small shelter, something to block the wind and it will have to be well anchored." Harold looked around more closely. "There are some holes drilled into the rock, see right here and over there. Somebody thought of this before us."

"Makes sense Dad, who knows how long the natives lived on this island."

"I am also thinking this lookout is tied to the storm shelter, since the trail connects them together with the village. This must be how they knew the big storms were coming. When they saw one, they ran down to the village and warned them."

Richard said, "Or they could have lighted a smokey fire and went down to join them in the storm shelter."

Harold was getting excited, "Yes, that was probably it. They may have kept a watch up here all the time, or at least at the time in the year when the storms could come."

Richard looked thoughtful, "I wonder if they had a better spot to get out of the wind. If they didn't have to be looking, like at night. Maybe just off the top, there may be a better camping spot."

Together they searched the peak top. Harold looking down over the edge said, "There, see between those two big rocks, the little flat area."

Richard found traces of a trail. They carefully made their way down to the camping spot. Once they were standing between the boulders, they turned and saw someone had craved a small cave into the side of the rock. Harold pointed into it, "There is where they spent the nights. This is great, all we need are some sleeping mats and blankets."

Richard looked thoughtful. "We need somewhere to keep the wood dry. I am thinking we will need a lot of wood for the beacon fire."

"Excellent point Son. We will store it here, until we have enough. Then we bring up the mats and blankets."

They hiked back down the trail and were home in time for lunch. Everybody was excited. The girls had gathered oysters and some other things. They had a great lunch and Harold told them about the pond with the waterfall they had discovered.

Alexandria and Amelia looked at each other with disappointment that their secret was out. Alexandria said, "You guys found the pond too?"

Harold was surprised, "Wow, you girls really get around. You weren't worried about going into the cave?"

Amelia asked, "What cave?"

Harold said, "The cave the pond is in. Wait a minute, you found a pond not in a cave?"

The girls looked at each other and wondered what to do. Alexandria finally said, "We were going to keep it a secret for a little while. Our resort comes with a pool. We went swimming this morning and the waterfall makes a great shower. Our pond is just upstream from where we get our water. Where is yours?"

Harold thought this over, "You will have to show us this pond of yours. Ours is up the mountain trail a little bit. A cave with a pond and waterfall. There is also a storm shelter. It looks like the natives used part of the cave to shelter in, if there was a hurricane."

Alexandria smirked, "So if I show you mine, will you show me yours?"

Harold was about to say 'yes' when he got the joke and sputtered. "Ah, uh, yes dear, just not in front of the children."

Alexandria smiled. "I could take just you there this afternoon and give you a private showing."

Amelia with mocked indignation said, "Hey, just remember where our drinking water comes from!"

After lunch, Alexandria led Harold out towards the pond. Harold turned and said, "We will be back before dinner."

A couple of hours later, they came back holding hands. Alexandria was wearing an orchid behind her left ear. They were in a very good mood. Harold smiled, "You kids ready for a hike to the cave pond?"

Amelia was excited, "Yes!"

They hiked up to the cave and the girls were amazed. They led them in on the pathway over the bridge to the pond. Alexandra took one look, "I think we went to the wrong pond Harold." She went down on one knee and put her hand in the water. "Nope, we made the right decision. This water is much colder."

Harold smiled, "Yes that is why this cave has such good natural air conditioning. If we want to get away from the heat, we can come up here. But the best part is over here." He led her over to the living area. "Here is our storm shelter."

Alexandria looked it over, "Yes, we can make some more sleeping mats, keep some blankets here, we could be very comfortable. I like the stove." She said as she pointed.

Harold looked, "I missed that. Looks like we now have a summer home by the lake."

Chapter Eleven

The next morning after breakfast, they all hiked up to the peak. Harold and Richard carried backpacks filled with firewood which made the climb much harder. They struggled a bit making it to the top. As they caught their breath at the top, the girls marveled at the view. Amelia enthusiastically pointed, "I can see the other islands!"

Richard managed to catch up to his breath first, "Yes, we don't know if anybody is over there. But they should be able to see our fire at night."

Alexandria longingly looked at the distant islands, "So close and yet so far away. I could almost reach out and touch them. But they may as well be on the moon."

Harold put his hand on her shoulder, more to steady himself then to comfort her. "Anyone there will be able to see our beacon fire. Then they will know we are here."

They stored the wood in the small cave and headed back down. Richard asked Harold, "Do you want to run another load of wood up this afternoon?"

Harold sourly replied, "No, guess I am showing my age, tomorrow morning will be soon enough for me."

Alexandria and Amelia starting weaving the new sleeping mats and things for the summer house. While

Harold and Richard carried wood up to the peak each day. After a few days the summer house was set up, and they had enough wood at the peak for the fire. To Harold's surprise, Alexandria and Amelia insisted on going.

After dinner, they gathered up a few things, put them in the two large backpacks and started hiking up. They took the firewood from the little cave and stacked enough for a good fire. In the little cave they put their sleeping mats and blankets. As the sun was starting to set, Harold pulled out a wooden bowl, packed with dried grass, surrounding ash, and coals from the dinner fire. He pulled back the grass and used a small stick to stir the coals. He blew gently on them and one glowed bright orange. He carefully fed it some of the dried grass and a flame appeared. It lit the grass, and he had a fire going in the wood bowl. He slowly dumped the bowl over a pile of small pieces of wood and set a few on top of the flames. The fire burned and got bigger. The large wood pieces were stacked around it. The flames grew higher.

Harold sat back and looked at the sun starting to go behind the horizon. "Looks like we timed this just right. We will let it burn like this and then add more wood once it is darker."

They all watched the sunset as it set behind the distant islands. Once it was down, the stars began to come out. None of them had seem the night sky from the peak before. The starry sky was so big, it felt if you were to let go of the ground, you could fall into it. The stars reached from one distant horizon to the other with nothing in-between. The Milky Way stretched out above them so vast, they knew they were looking into the bottomless depths of space. Harold spoke reverently, "You can't see this and not be moved by it."

Richard asked, "What do you see Dad?"

"What God has made and how small we and the earth are, and yet all this would mean nothing without us to see it."

Richard was puzzled, "What do you mean?"

Harold pointed at the sky, "If you made all of this, wouldn't you want someone to see it? What is an artist without anyone to appreciate his paintings? If you can make this, you would want to share it. I think we are meant to see this because we can appreciate it. One of the ways how we differ from the animals and why we are here."

Richard was surprised. "Pretty profound Dad, never thought of you as the religious type."

"I'm not. But seeing this, it makes you think."

"This sounds like it is new to you, Dad."

"Yes, it is, I never took the time to really look up and think. Our old world was designed to keep us from thinking. Just look at all the nonsense we used to believe. It kept us so busy we didn't have time to think and indoctrinated us with what they wanted us to think.

Maybe this is why there is so much light pollution, to keep us from seeing this and thinking about it. But here on this island, we are free of it all and we can truly see the heavens if we look."

"Dad, with this view I can't argue. I do agree with appreciating it. I have taken too much for granted, what we have been through, has opened my eyes. I think all of us has been rethinking our lives. Sometimes I wonder if we should have lighted this fire. Maybe we are better off where we are. I don't want to go back. I don't want to go back to what I was. I don't know if I could resist the indoctrination twenty-four seven, being surrounded in it and force fed it."

Harold shrugged. "I wonder too if we are making the right choice. But it is dangerous for us to be so isolated. What if we needed medical attention? If nothing else, our clothes will wear out as they are doing, and I don't fancy wearing a grass skirt. But you do make a good point."

They kept the fire burning most of the night and took turns sleeping in the small cave shelter. In the morning they all watched the sun come up. It was spectacular. But as they were watching it, Richard noticed something, "Dad, look at the waves."

Harold turned and looked around at the waves hitting the reef. "They are huge, and they seem to be coming from the west, like the big storm did."

Richard pointed to the west. "I can't see any dark clouds."

Harold looked, "The storm is still over the horizon."

"Must be a pretty big storm."

Harold was very concerned. "I think we may have discovered how the natives knew when a hurricane was coming."

Richard was shocked, "I hate to say it, but I think you are right. How much time do we have?"

"Depends on how fast it is moving, maybe a few days, maybe less."

Alexandria said, "Let's get back home and pack. We should gather food too."

They packed up their sleeping mats and headed back down the trail. By the time they were nearing the storm cave, the wind had started to pick up. Harold said, "It is getting closer."

They dropped off their sleeping things in the cave and headed down to the house. They gathered up what they wanted to take with them and did a quick gathering of fruit. Once their backpacks were all loaded, they headed up to the cave as the winds increased. As they hiked up through the jungle, the trees started swaying. By the time they were clear of the jungle, leaves were blowing past them. It was getting difficult to walk on the trail out in the open. With nothing to block the wind, it kept trying to blow them off the trail. Harold took his wife's hand and led her along as they struggled up towards the cave. Eventually they turned into the little valley. The wind was now blocked. They walked into the cave. Once inside, they turned and looked back. Outside the sky was beginning to get dark as the clouds were rolling in. Not the white fluffy ones, but the big dark rainy ones.

The walk to the back of the cave was surprisingly calm. Harold could tell there was more air movement in the cave, but not all that much more. Once they reached their summer house, they set out their sleeping mats and set things up. Harold got a small fire going to keep hot coals on hand. They talked and relaxed as the light from the skylight gradually grew dimmer.

They ate lunch and listened apprehensively to the sound of the wind outside as it increased to a roar. The rain was now very heavy with a waterfall from the skylight which poured into the cave lake. The cave waterfall also increased. The stream flowing from the lake increased in volume as well. Above the roaring wind and pouring rain, they could hear the sounds of heavy thunder. Bright flashes of lighting could be seen through the skylight in the sky above. The storm raged on for the rest of the day and into the night. They bedded down for the night with the warm glow of a small fire.

Sunlight lighted up the cave in the morning. Harold got up and walked over the edge of the pool. He looked up out through the small skylight and saw the blue sky. The storm was over. Once everyone was up, they had breakfast, and walked to the cave entrance.

At the entrance everything looked the same. They walked out through the small valley, came around the turn and looked out at the jungle below them. The jungle was gone. It looked like a badly mown lawn. Most of the trees were down or stripped of their leaves. The palm trees survived while many other trees did not. The rocky slopes of the peak were covered with windblown leaves. They were stunned by the destruction. In silence they walked down the trail toward their house. Once they reached the jungle, they had to step and climb over fallen branches and trees. They made it to their house and found the frame stripped of the thatching. Harold looked it over, "We can replace the thatching," he looked around, "plenty of material to work with."

Richard looked at the trees, "Finding fruit may be difficult."

Alexandria added, "The waves probably washed away the oysters."

Harold said, "Maybe, maybe not. Let's go see what we have left."

They walked down to the beach which looked very different. The waves and the wind had moved the sand far up onto the shore. Even the rocks were partly covered. They went to look for oysters. Alexandria searched the tidal pools. "I don't see any. They must be buried under all this sand."

Harold looked too. "They will probably work their way up through the sand. They must be used to this sort of thing, or they would have gone extinct a long time ago."

Richard stepped close to his dad. "Things are not looking so good. What do you think we should do?"

Harold smiled, "I think we should all wave to the guy in the boat!" He shouted as he pointed out at the entrance to the bay. A boat was entering the bay. It was an open boat with an outboard motor. The guy piloting it, headed straight for the beach and drove it up onto the sand. The guy said, "I saw your signal fire before the storm. I thought I should come over and check to see if you needed any help."

Harold said, "Yes, we certainly do. Our plane crashed here months ago. We have been marooned here since then."

The boat guy asked, "You want a ride back to the island I came from?"

Harold said, "Yes, we would like that very much."

They got in the boat, and he took them across the sea to the other island. The waves were still on the large size from the hurricane. The boat rode up one wave after another. At the crest of each one, they could look ahead and see where they were going or look back at where they had come from. Harold noticed his family was mostly looking back.

The boat guy said, "My name is Maui Pulu."

Harold said, "Harold Rock."

Maui's eyes got big. "You're the missing billionaire. Everybody been looking for you, but not here. You are supposed to be around Hawaii. How did you end up here?"

Harold rolled his eyes, "We had a particularly talented pilot who was very good at getting lost."

Maui smiled, "I would say so. No one even thought to look for you on Bird Island."

Harold asked, "Bird Island?"

Maui focused on steering the boat into the next wave. "Not official name. Some of us locals call it that. There's a legend people once lived there, but they became too many and ate all the animals. They over fished the bay and ate everything they could find, until they had no choice but to leave the island. The only thing left on the island was the birds."

Harold thought about it, "We did find remains of a village, and we never saw any animals on the island other than birds. I think your legend is true."

The boat was now approaching an island. Maui headed in through an opening in the reef and entered a large lagoon. He headed over to a small wooden pier that had seen better days. He tied up the boat and said, "Welcome to the Island of Nowhere, not an official name, but it stuck. We don't have a hotel. You will stay with me. That house there is mine."

A woman stood in the open doorway waving. Maui said, "That is my wife Amataga. She will be happy to see you."

Amataga was indeed very happy to see them and made them feel right at home. Maui explained, "I should take you to the store. The owner has a satellite phone. You can let people know you are still alive."

Harold nearly jumped out of his seat. "Great idea, let's go."

It was dinner time by the time Harold came back with Maui. Alexandria asked, "Harold, what took so long to make a phone call?"

Harold smiled, "Many phone calls. We are all dead by the way. Took a while to get that straighten out. I also had to set up some lines of credit. We have one at the store. I also did some shopping. I bought Bird Island."

Everyone was silent for a moment, and then Amelia shouted, "Yes! Dad bought the island!"

Alexandria was puzzled. "Why did you buy the island?"

Harold looked thoughtful, "The sale is still pending, we could still backout."

Alexandria looked Harold right in the eye, "I will divorce you in a heartbeat, if you backout."

Richard said, "We would be fools to live anywhere else."

Maui said, "Amataga, we got new neighbors."

Amataga ran in from the kitchen and gave everybody a big hug.

Later over the dinner table, Harold explained, "I am going to hire Maui, if you're interested in the job, as our delivery guy." Maui nodded his head and looked at his wife and smiled.

Harold continued, "I am looking into hiring an architect to design and build us a new house on the island. We will be looking for local workers for construction." Maui nodded his head again. "With the credit line at the store, we can buy the things we need, like new clothes."

Amataga said very firmly, "Until your house is built, you stay with us."

Chapter Twelve

Harold stood on the stone pier waiting for Maui to bring the boat alongside. Harold grabbed the rope Maui tossed him and tied up the boat. "Welcome Captain, Pulu. It is very good to see you, my friend."

Maui stepped off the boat and gave Harold a bear hug. "That is from Amataga. She wanted me to thank you for the set of dishes you surprised her with. She just loves them. Heaven help me if a break one."

A man stepped onto the pier next to Maui. Harold reached out and shook his hand warmly. "Bob, it is so good to see you, it has been such a long time."

Bob looked around, "Harold, pleasure to see you again in person. I has been over a year since I saw you in the office boss."

Harold smiled, "Well, as you can see, I work remotely, very remotely in fact."

Bob agreed, "I didn't realize just how remote you were until I got here. I think you win the prize for most remote, remote worker."

Harold turned to Maui. "Do you want to stay over or go back?"

Maui pointed over his shoulder. "I have to go back, my wife's rules, I don't get to stay over unless she does too."

Harold laughed and padded Maui on the shoulder. "Smart wife. She is welcome anytime."

They said their goodbyes and then Harold led Bob toward the house. As they walked through the jungle, Bob saw a thatched old style island house. "Very well-matched home for the setting,"

Harold said, "That is an improved version of the first house we built on the island ourselves. It was damaged in a hurricane. We liked it so much, with the help of local craftsmen, we built better so it should survive any future hurricanes. We use it as our beach house and for guests."

They walked through the jungle and started up the slope. Bob pointed to a house up ahead that looked very traditional and very modern at the same time. "This is our new house. Fully energy independent and hurricane proof. We built it up here to avoid any flying trees in a hurricane and to get a better view. We also connected it to a cave we discovered which contains the main freshwater spring for this side of the island, which helps keep the house cool. Natural air conditioning, running water and a kitchen with modern conveniences. That is the garden over there, we irrigate it with the water from the spring, and we have a fish pond."

After dinner, Bob sat at the table with the Rocks. He asked, "Harold this is an amazing place, but I have to ask, why do you stay here. I would have thought after your plane crashed here. The first thing you would have wanted to do was to get off this island, not live here forever."

Harold smiled, "We wanted to stay here, because this is as far from San Franisco and the woke culture as we could get."

Bob was puzzled. "I can understand wanting to get out of San Fransico, as you know we had to move the company out. But what is so bad about being woke?"

Harold looked more serious, "It is a poison, Bob. It nearly killed all of us. It was ruining all of our lives and our family. You know how it was choking the business."

Bob rolled his eyes, "I wish it was past tense. But it is just something we just have live with."

Harold said, "It is more than that, it is like living with poison in the air. You need to reject poison. Here on this island, we found ourselves and each other. We are now a close-knit family. Before, we hardly knew each other. Being here, we avoid so many problems."

Bob looked over at Richard, "Richard, how do you feel about living here?"

Richard took a breath, "It saved my life. Dad and being here, changed my life. I never want to go back to what I was before. When I told my girlfriend, she laughed her head off, she thought I was joking. I was so embarrassed, she realized I was serious, then she was stunned. She still can't wrap her head around how messed up our old world is. She grew up out here and can't understand what is going on in the states."

Alexandria added, "Most here either don't know, or don't believe it. Those that do, think it is either mass insanity or a Chinese plot to make America look stupid and morally bankrupt."

Bob asked Amelia, "Don't you miss everything back home, school, your friends going places?"

Amelia looked sour as she thought about it, "No, not at all. I didn't have any real friends there. Everyone was too selfish and wrapped up in themselves. School was awful, a real woke indoctrination camp. I am so happy I escaped from all that. We go to the best places here. A walk on the island is a walk in a tropical paradise. We also visit some of the other islands. But best of all, I have my family. We were all strangers before."

Harold added, "We have become part of the local community, and it is not just like neighbors, it is more like an extended family. Certainly not without its problems, but far better than what we left behind."

Bob thought about it, "Sounds like you have discovered paradise."

Harold smiled, "Yes, and we would be fools to leave it."

Bob asked, "Don't you think someday things will change and You will want to come back?"

Harold frowned. "No, wokeism is the same path the Romans were on. It destroyed them. I don't believe there is a path back. Many in the community of American expatriates feel the same way. Once a society puts same sex relationships on a par with marriage, morality is going extinct. What we see in the woke world are the last traces of morality and family being attacked and destroyed. If I expressed these opinions openly in American, they would attack me and try to cancel me. They are burning their bridges, and the poison is spreading to the rest of the world.

Bob was surprised, "But what would you do if it comes here?"

Harold said, "That is why I bought the island. To give us as much time and distance as I could. Time to for us to strengthen our family and ourselves to have the moral strength to resist the flood of woke immoral degeneracy."

Bob asked, "So in the end, each of you will become an island of morality?"

Harold said, "It is that or drown in wokeism. Together as a family and with likeminded people, each of us will be a beacon of sanity in an insane world. But everyone has a choice to make, to choose to be a moral person or an immoral person."

Bob pointed out, "You make it sound so black and white. Everyone just needs to get along and accept people as they are."

Harold responded, "I accept that everyone makes a choice, I just don't approve of the choices some people make. They make theirs and I make mine. But the woke are not content with that, with them, you are free to make any choice if it agrees with theirs."

Bob suppressed a laugh, "Yes, that seems to be the biggest problem. A complete intolerance of any opinion or standard which clashes with their own. It is an increasing problem in the office."

Harold got serious, "That is part of the reason why I wanted you to come out here. I wanted to talk to you in person, to get your viewpoint on some changes. I want to make to company policy to take a firmer hand on woke activism in the workplace."

Bob looked hard at Harold, "That would really set them off. They make enough trouble as it is."

"It is to be expected. But if we ignore it, it will only get worse. If we let them, they will take over the company as they have at other companies. We can't let them dictate company policy. We will have to work out the details while you are here. I am thinking of setting of rules for firing woke activists who make trouble in the company."

Bob was concerned, "They will turn on us."

"Of course, but they will cause much less trouble if they are outside the company than if they are inside. I think if we do this, we can make the company a much better place to work at. If no one, has to be concerned about triggering hypersensitive people, who think their feelings are far more important than anyone else's. They may actually be able to focus on getting some work done."

Bob was alarmed, "You just can't fire people for being woke."

"No of course not. Only if they make an issue of it and are disruptive. It really is basic common business sense. Keep the people who make you money and get rid of the ones who don't. We are a business, not a charity."

Bob smiled, "What a novel thought, a business is for making money. Sounds like old school has become new school."

Harold grinned, "Yes, a cutting-edge way of being profitable, cut away the fat. I don't care what a person's personal beliefs are. They are none of my business. But if they try to make them part of my business, they must go. Activism is incompatible with profitability since activism is the pursuit of political goals instead of financial ones. Any company that succumbs to activism will become less profitable. If the growing cancer of activism is not removed, it will in time, take over the company and kill it."

Bob agreed, "You are right of course, but like fighting cancer, it will not be easy."

Harold was firm, "It is a life and death struggle for the survival of my company. We both know of other companies with this problem, some have died, and others are dying. Unless they take drastic action and remove the cancer killing them, they are doomed. I will not let the cancer that nearly destroyed my family, destroy my company."

Bob turned and looked out the window at the setting sun. "You are right, and I agree with you. I support you fully in taking action to save the company. Just as the sun is going down, I hope we can root out the cancer and send the activists off into the sunset."

"I am glad you are with me on this. I believe it really is our biggest threat. Now that the sun is going down, I want to take you outside and show you the stars."

Bob was puzzled, "What is so important about the stars?"

Harold stood up and gestured towards the window, "You may not have really seen the stars. Let me show them to you."

Bob followed Harold out the door as his family followed behind them. Bob said, "I don't see what the big deal is, I have seen the stars before."

Harold pointed up. Bob looked up and his mouth fell open. After a while he said, "I didn't know there were so many. It is amazing and humbling at the same time."

Harold put his hand on Bob's shoulder. "It means a lot to me Bob, that you are the sort of person who can really see the stars. Far too many people look but don't see. They are blind to the great beauty surrounding us in the real world."

Bob still looking up, asked, "Why is this important?"

"Because it takes an open mind to see it."

Made in the USA
Monee, IL
04 February 2025

a3aedf33-8066-4f2b-ad02-e779fa93a3cbR01